THE BORDER JUMPERS

THE BORDER JUMPERS

Will C. Brown

Chivers Press • G.K. Hall & Co.
Bath, Avon, England • Thorndike, Maine USA

This Large Print edition is published by Chivers Press, England, and by G.K. Hall & Co., USA.

Published in 1996 in the U.K. by arrangement with C. S. Boyles Jr. c/o the Golden West Literary Agency.

Published in 1996 in the U.S. by arrangement with Golden West Literary Agency.

U.K. Hardcover   ISBN 0–7451–4832–8   (Chivers Large Print)
U.K. Softcover   ISBN 0–7451–4843–3   (Camden Large Print)
U.S. Softcover   ISBN 0–7838–1738–X (Nightingale Collection Edition)

The text of this Large Print edition is unabridged.
Other aspects of the book may vary from the original edition.

Set in 16 pt. New Times Roman.

Printed in Great Britain on acid-free paper.

British Library Cataloguing in Publication Data available

Library of Congress Cataloging-in-Publication Data

Brown, Will C., 1905–
    The border jumpers / by Will C. Brown.
        p. cm.
    ISBN 0–7838–1738–X (lg. print : sc)
    1. Large type books.   I. Title.
[PS3552.R739B67   1996]
813′.54—dc20   96–10392

CHAPTER ONE

The first part of the journey seemed like no time at all. There were Lucy's shining eyes and the kids' excited faces to start him off and fair put wings on the hours, to say nothing of this honor from the neighbors. Made a good feeling, to think that out of all the men they had picked Lincoln Jones for the long trip. They had entrusted him with their money and the mission, a pleasurable distinction for a man, a sign that he amounted to something in the world.

Under him were the rhythmic muscles of his best horse, and up there were lazy flocks of April clouds topping the Texas morning. Before the sun had set twice in the loneliness behind him he made Bitter Creek. He stabled his horse in the wagon yard there against his return, and another night of riding up beside the driver on the high rickety perch of the stagecoach put him in the railhead of Crosscut at midmorning.

The stage journey ended, Lincoln and the driver stretched cramped legs in the dusty side street, feeling almost like old acquaintances after the night of rambling talk.

The driver squinted up at him in a final tally. Lincoln was a grave man, except for the offer of friendliness in the back of his dark eyes; a

1

durable man with the brown, indestructible look of the prairie-bred.

The driver said, 'I keep thinkin' I seen you before.'

A lot of men had hard bony faces and Comanche-dark eyes. Lincoln said affably, 'You might have. Then again, I reckon not.'

'Sure seems like I have, somewheres.'

'Expect you see a lot of people, easy to get 'em mixed up. You know what time the train leaves here?'

'One o'clock. That's if the engine ain't broke down. Ridin' it or just want to see it pull out?'

'I'm riding it. Going to Fort Worth.'

'It'll bounce the livin' hell out of you. But you hit the right day. It comes in and goes back just twice a week.'

'I know. That's why I planned to get here today. Well, so long, driver.'

'Good luck, Odessa. Look out for train bandits.' The driver chuckled and turned to go about his unloading.

Lincoln hoisted his valise and headed for the main street.

Crosscut looked as if it might have been hauled in on the new railroad and tossed out in a hurry. To a man of discernment, there were ample signs that sin in quantity was pushing west with the railroad. The store fronts were unpainted, but he could see red aplenty in men's eyes and on women's cheeks. They and the shacks and saloons all looked like they

2

could do with a good scrubbing of ashes and currycomb.

Unaccustomed to the dusty maelstrom of foot, horse, buggy, and wagon movements, he paused uncertainly at the corner to take in the street and get his bearings. The remark of the stage driver lingered, and before he could put it out of his mind it started a small chain of imaginations. Why would the old man think he had seen him before?

The boom-town scene rekindled recollections, and then he forcibly hazed them all back into the herd of the forgotten. These people were not looking at him. It was only his damn-fool imagination. In the isolated Odessa country there was a feeling of security in the isolation itself. Here, there were people. And where there were people, a man from a lonely land would naturally feel conspicuous until he got used to it.

Lucy's last whispered admonition came plainly again to his ear: *Don't be afraid!*

He stopped a man, inquired the way to the depot, thanked the man briefly, and moved on.

As he wandered watchfully along the plank sidewalks, Lincoln felt thankful that Lucy and the kids didn't live where they had to wake to commotion and sights like this every sunrise. He gave due appreciation to this and filed it away in his mind as another of his several blessings.

Out at Odessa, the Texas spaces were

3

cleansed in their own vastness and even if it almost never rained, nature had a way of sprucing up each new day with the starlight wash of the old and the peaceful smell of sage and Indian paintbrush. Odessa lay near to the Pecos. Folks to the east were apt to say what a wild country it was, out there, with rough people. But to Lincoln the far land beyond the thin blue haze of the Tonkawas had been like a clean bandage to raw wounds. The old scars were gone. The Odessa prairies had been a salve of peace.

Here in Crosscut, his nostrils were offended by the smell of street dust and sweat, whisky-sweet batwing doorways, and finally by a strange, sinister odor that at first he could not fix.

Valise dangling from his long left arm, shoulders slightly stooped in his muscle-binding Sunday coat to compensate his angular height to high-kneed stride, and squinted prairieman's eyes working alertly ahead, he followed directions toward the depot and found the unholy odor coming to meet him.

Then he knew what it was.

His skin slackened on the long bones of his cheeks and the sun-etched smile crinkles of his mouth deepened a little in expectancy. He had seen a locomotive only once before in his life, but he remembered.

Bound to be the mesquite wood burning

4

under the engine boiler. Wood in that firebox didn't smell like wood burning in the open, or anywhere else. Lincoln had talked with a few people who had ridden on a train and had lugged wood for it at the fuel stops, and he had never known one with a good word to say for the noisy contraption.

You not only got to ride that thing, he told himself in wry good humor. *You got to smell that stinking boiler all the way to Fort Worth, then all the way back!*

Curiosity to see the train was strong within him, but so was dread. Suddenly he felt a hesitancy to come face to face with it and he had time to spare. He told himself that he should clean up a little and eat a good meal before getting on the train. The trip would take all afternoon, all the night, and most of the next day, to make the two hundred and fifty miles to Fort Worth. Even if the thing didn't break down. He turned a corner before he reached the depot and located the washroom at the rear of a new pine hotel.

He dipped water from a keg into the granite washpan. After a brief deliberation he removed his holstered Colt and stuffed it, with his gun belt, into his valise. This he did reluctantly, but conscientious of his promise. Lucy had declared that it was not proper for a man to wear his gun on a train, nor in a big city like Fort Worth. He was going to a civilized country, she had insisted. Not like the wild

5

Odessa frontier. She had thought that the worn holster and heavy .45 might better be left entirely, but they had compromised on his taking it off before he got on the train.

From the valise he pulled the money belt of soft canvas with the neighbors' six hundred dollars in it. His hard hands went over the bulges made by the currency. That money meant a lot, to a lot of people, and again he felt pride in being the one entrusted with it. Dollars were scarce at Odessa.

He replaced the money in the bottom of the valise, pushing his spare clothing down firmly upon it. It would be as safe there, if he kept his eye on the valise, as buckled around his middle, and a heap more comfortable.

He soaked his face at the basin, stooping his long joints to the wash bench, then took a razor from the valise and shaved with soapsuds and cold water. He beat some of the dust off his clothes and ordered his crow-black hair with a snaggle-toothed comb. He took tally of the sun-darkened features in the mirror, and chuckled shortly. Couldn't get the hard-times signs off that face, for there they'd been all his years, which were near to thirty. Lucy had said that Fort Worth sure would see a handsome man, but he doubted that. Just a wife's way of sending a man off feeling prideful.

Not that he was old. Out where he came from, time was apt to hand a man two years of aging for one on the calendar. But he could try to reset the expression a little, to a shape not so grim, and did so. He also straightened the stoop out of his hard-muscled shoulders, though he was permanently saddle-bent and his legs too long for any semblance of graceful stance afoot.

A man swung in, heavy-booted and pushing up a dilapidated hat as he entered, his holstered gun brushing the door edge. The suddenness of his entry into the washroom brought Lincoln around in the alertness developed in far and lonely places, where a man was wise to respond to any unexpected movement with quick appraisal. The room felt too cramped for his size and overcrowded.

The man no more than glanced up at him, and Lincoln picked up his valise, said, 'Howdy,' and departed.

The sun's position tallied with the first touch of nooning hunger in the hard lean middle under his belt. How or whether a man would eat on a train was a mystery. It seemed prudent to him that he fortify himself while he had the chance. He walked in the metallic sheen of sunlight bouncing off all the new lumber until he sighted a sign that said: *New York Café*.

Again he had the momentary impression of unwarranted intrusion, as when the man had come into the washroom. It had been a long time since he had eaten in a place like this. Everywhere he turned, looked like, there were people. It would take a little time to get used to

7

that. Eating at a counter where men were crowded in right and left, elbows and wrists and jaws working like a row of blackbirds on a fence, was an unaccustomed experience. Yet, there was an aura of excitement in so much bustle. It spoke of a town that was busy building itself, and of the whole state of Texas standing up and stretching its muscles in all directions, reaching into its unused distances with a thrust of railroad steel, sending people westward where people in any numbers had never been seen before.

He sat on an uncomfortable stool, the precious valise locked between his black half boots, assaulted by the many sounds and movements. He ate heartily—fried steak, lumpy, warm potatoes, pepper-tracked gravy and biscuits big as his hands, and coffee so belligerent that he concluded it might have broken out of anything lighter than the crockery mug imprisoning it. He put down a silver half-dollar in pay, then headed for the train.

At the south end of main street stood the depot, still unpainted and the farthest west real estate of the Fort Worth & Chihuahua Railroad Company. Lincoln circled the structure, then stopped and gave a good look at the thing that smoked and moaned on the hot steel rails.

In the same moment of his sudden halt, a woman almost bumped into him.

She nimbly side-stepped, averting a bodily impact by inches, and hurried along, her small black shoes flashing.

''Scuse me, ma'am.'

She did not glance back, and he had only passing notice of powdered face beneath a dressy travel veil, the swish of her long-skirted suit, and the faint trailing smell of perfume that was pleasant to his nostrils, even with the train smell rising to high heaven. With the smoking engine to claim his attention, he still caught the pleasing lines of the woman's movements, the businesslike approach she made to the depot window, where she put down her suitcase and opened her hand purse for ticket money. City-dressed woman. She knew what she was about, not timid from people or trains. Lucy would have been scared to death, as what Odessa woman wouldn't, taking off alone on a long train trip. Not that this thought was disparaging to them. The woman buying the ticket and laughing now with the depot man, how would *she* look, waiting in the weedy corner of the cabin's rail fence, like Lucy that time, with an eye along the barrel of a twenty-pound rifle, her husband riding range five miles away, two kids in the house behind her, and the dogs bristling at the distant sounds of a horse-stealing Comanche band across Turkey Creek? With this idle comparison resolved in favor of Lucy and all the Odessa settlers' wives, Lincoln took time to study the train once more.

'Taking a trip? What'd you think of it?'

'Ugly danged thing,' Lincoln said fervently.

Then, not wishing to offend any Crosscutter who might be a little particular about the train, he turned and squinted down good-naturedly at the man who had spoken. 'But I reckon it wasn't bred for beauty.'

The man, flabby in the neck and stomach, had pale eyes that dodged about like cottontails in underbrush. Small tufts of pinkish hair studded each ear and he talked jumpily, as if each word hurt his mouth.

''Bout time to get on. By gaddly, we got a long, rough ride ahead. Going to Fort Worth? You must be from out west of here.'

'Odessa.'

The flabby one wore a green striped suit and stained gray fedora, and a tarnished yellow stickpin in his polkadot shirt front. He seemed friendly enough.

'Long ways, Odessa.'

Lincoln said, 'That's right. Going to Fort Worth.'

The pale eyes halted momentarily to examine the tall prairieman as a poker player might take a second tally of his cards, and then darted into the underbrush again.

'Bet you never rode a train before. Well, you stick with me, friend, and I'll show you the ropes. Always glad to help out a feller.'

He started to say more, but his glance scooted past Lincoln. He mumbled something

10

profane and moved jerkily away.

Lincoln looked back. A lanky man with guns sagging on each leg and a battered town marshal's star on his blue shirt leaned against the depot wall. He picked his teeth and looked scowlingly at nothing.

As Lincoln hesitated, the lawman came loosely into motion and ambled over.

'That a friend of yours? Where you from?'

'Odessa, Texas.' Lincoln started to say more, to tell the lawman that he was on a fairly important mission to Fort Worth. But he refrained, deciding it would sound like making himself important.

Or was it the law badge that made him uncomfortable? The tension came back to him, as it had when he first walked in the streets of the boom town. It had been a long time since he had seen a law badge.

The marshal spat speculatively, slouched with his thumbs in his belt, and allowed a grin to form.

'Gentleman from Odessa, huh?'

'Depends on how you mean it, marshal.'

'Some places it's a polite way of calling a man a son of—'

'I know about that.'

'Well, no offense meant.'

'None taken. It's all right when you say it friendly.' Lincoln felt an itch to get away. The marshal was looking him over.

'I ever seen you some place before?'

'I reckon not.'

'Mind if I ask you your name?'

He looked the marshal in the eye and said shortly, 'Name's Smith. Bob Smith.'

The lawman's eyes shifted and with them his thoughts also seemed to change direction. Lincoln turned.

He saw the flabby pale-eyed man hustling up the steps of the coach, not looking back.

'I'd watch out for strangers, if I was you. But you look able to take care of yourself.'

The marshal scowled. Lincoln nodded, said, '*Adios*, marshal,' and stalked to the depot window.

He bought his ticket and trudged across the dusty loading area. People were lounging and looking. A fat man in overalls climbed familiarly into the rumbling innards of the high-waisted engine. Behind the engine were two cattle cars, baggage car, coach, and caboose. A brass bell, giving off dazzling sun flashes, began to throw out a clamor awful to the ears. An unexpected whistle toot, within an eruption of black smoke, jolted Lincoln's whole body as if an invisible steer had butted him.

Swinging his valise, he climbed the high steps of the wooden coach. To his left was the end door of the baggage car, now closed. To his right was the open door to the coach, and beyond that the seats where he would ride this noisy bronc for many a long hour. Before

12

entering, he took a glance back at the depot, and straight away saw the marshal. The lawman looked at him. They held the glance trading between them for a moment, then the marshal turned his head. A man carrying a rifle crooked under his arm came into Lincoln's view, and it was to this one the lawman had transferred his attention.

The car seemed dark, in contrast to the midday glare outside. He saw that there were few passengers, maybe half a dozen. He selected a seat and settled himself on the hard red plush, and waited tensely, as he might have awaited the first mad plunge of a wild horse newly saddled and mounted.

Eventually, by jerks and steamy straining, the train started. The depot, the grinning spectators, the scowling city marshal, crawled by and out of vision. Crosscut seemed to stagger back into the distance, retreating from the noise, until Lincoln saw nothing from his window but smoke and empty land wastes scrambling past.

This was the start, at last.

He grinned to himself, liking it, finding the speed and rail screechings exhilarating, and wished that Lucy and the two children could see him now. There would come a time, though, when everybody would ride like this. Texas was moving west, no doubt about it. The whole South was getting itself put back together. Some day the rails would cross the

13

Tonkawa hills and twist through the Van Horn mounds, pick up the banks of the Rio Grande, and go all the way into El Paso. The Odessa country would grow, too, and he would have a sizable herd by then, barring misfortune, and his cattle would be going to market from railroad loading pens.

In that moment of his lush speculation, he abruptly remembered how he had lied to the marshal about his name.

Why would he do that? He bitterly resolved that he would never let himself do it again. If he was a coward, he should have stayed in the wild land and let them send Fez Duncan on the trip, Fez having been itching for the job but getting no support.

And this made a strange mixture of emotions within him, as if his pleasure in the trip and his dread of it were two distinct things daring one another to cross a fighting line down in his chest. The rush of the train eastward like a scared jack rabbit was hustling him out of the only life he had ever known, one way he looked at it. But in an uneasy opposite feeling, he seemed to have been trapped and transported back to a time that had never quite gone. Yet, the valise in his lap was weighty reminder of his right to be here, and the six hundred dollars stood for the wishes of a dozen settler families and their favorable opinion of Lincoln Jones.

He turned back from the window. The

woman sat alone three seats ahead and across the aisle.

He could see a little of her white profile and found it agreeable to look at. Her veil was turned up now, over the hat which was small and close-fitting and spiced with a curling white feather. Her dark hair, almost black, showed above the feminine lines of neck and shoulders. He remembered the rustle of her skirts, back at the depot, and the perfume. She was young, younger than Lincoln by a few years, he judged, though it was difficult to estimate the age of a woman when she was decked out like that.

She turned her head and their eyes met.

The glance held for the seconds it took him to politely move his gaze elsewhere. It would be plain to her that he was taking her in, though he knew no particular care to do so. He got a quick impression of an inviting blue glance, perhaps a tinge too much of cheek paint, and pink lips. But that could be a new fashion he had not known about.

When the conductor took his ticket, he told Lincoln, as he had the men in the seats behind him, 'We'd like to have all able-bodied men help carry wood for the engine when we get to East Fork. More that help, quicker we'll get moving again.'

Lincoln nodded. 'Wood's already cut, I take it?' he said genially. The conductor said yep, all the men had to do was just tote it to the engine.

One of the men behind Lincoln two or three seats called in a heavy drawl that it would be worth carrying ten cords of wood just to get shed of the buckin' coach a spell.

The conductor moved on. The woman smiled up at him in a friendly way when she extended her ticket. The conductor took off his cap and held it under his arm, giving the transaction a special touch of elegance which Lincoln observed with favor. At that moment, the flabby man who had spoken with him at the depot stood up across the aisle, balanced precariously, and slid into the seat beside Lincoln.

'How you doing, Odessa?'

'All right. About to get the hang of riding this thing, now.'

'Lemme put that valise up in the rack,' the man said suddenly. 'You don't have to hold it. Safe up there, even if it was loaded with valuables. Now.' He pulled out a cigar and nibbled at the end of it. 'Been to Fort Worth before?'

'Not in a long time.'

'Cattle deal, I guess?'

'Not exactly.'

Lincoln thought the stranger was too inquisitive, yet it was not bad to have someone to make conversation with, and he saw no cause to offend him. He said, 'I'm on my way to hire a schoolteacher.'

'Teacher?' The rabbity eyes jumped back

16

and forth. 'What you want with a schoolteacher?'

'Folks around Odessa are sending me,' Lincoln said, hearing his own words with some feeling of immodesty. 'We're going to start a school.'

'A school, huh? Never thought about there being kids out in that country—thought it was too tough for anything but longhorns and outlaws.'

'Well, maybe it used to be,' Lincoln said. 'But there's enough of us out there now with kids that need schoolin', so we decided we better hire a teacher. They pitched in to send me to Fort Worth to find one.'

The flabby man shifted cigar, narrowed one restless eye, and peered hard at Lincoln.

'Takes a heap of money to get a teacher to move that far west. Reckon you're prepared to pay the price, eh?'

'We raised a fair amount.'

The cottontail eyes scurried up to the valise and back.

'Ummmm. Friend, my name's Beasley. Sam Beasley.' He did not extend a hand, but worried with the cigar. Lincoln spoke his own name.

'Well, now, Lincoln Jones, by gaddly, it's a strange thing. Very strange. Lucky, you might say, I just happen to know a schoolteacher in Fort Worth. Wants to move west, in fact.'

This was interesting and Lincoln told

17

him so.

'Yep.' Beasley's mouth-corner words were jumpy like his eyes. 'If you got the money I might help you make a deal.'

Lincoln took cautious stock of Beasley again. He remembered how the lawman at Crosscut had scowled at Beasley's retreating back.

'This teacher you know, man or woman?'

'She's a—He's a—Well, by gaddly, which did you have in mind?' Beasley ran the cigar back and forth rapidly.

'I reckon you mean,' Lincoln said, 'you know both kind?'

'I know a lot of people in Fort Worth,' Beasley said hurriedly. 'Just happens some are teachers. Be glad to help you make some contacts when we get there.'

'Well, that's right neighborly,' Lincoln allowed. He shifted comfortably, thinking of the Beasleys in the past. 'You know, Beasley, when I first saw you, I figured you'd be the caliber that'd help a stranger in Fort Worth. Especially a stranger with the money on him to pay the teacher a year in advance.'

Beasley's head cocked. Half-closed eyes squinted hard at the Odessa man but Lincoln's face was inscrutable. Lincoln let the flabby one take care of his own puzzlement in silence.

Beasley tried a knowing wink at the solemn face, accompanied by a light nudge of elbow. 'Lot of fancy women in Fort Worth.'

'Already know a fancy one,' Lincoln said.

'In Fort Worth?'

'No. At home. Name's Lucy. She's my wife.'

After a silence, Beasley said, 'Well, glad to of met you, Jones. See you in Fort Worth. Maybe you'd like for me to get you a room at the hotel where I'm going.'

'Might would,' Lincoln said.

Beasley extended a puffy white hand. A big, bony, callused hand closed upon it. Beasley's legs shot out and a convulsion seemed to rock him. He moaned. *'Gaddly!* That's no ax handle!'

Holding his right hand gingerly with his left, Beasley stumbled down the aisle.

An hour later, when next Lincoln noticed, he sighted Beasley in the vestibule between the coach and baggage car with the woman in the satin suit. He was a fellow to make acquaintances fast, Lincoln concluded. Beasley appeared to be doing all the talking and the woman all the listening.

He turned back to watching the sliding countryside, bleak and empty with the mesquite wastes cut by gullies and red sand ridges.

He remembered this country. This was the part of Texas everybody said God apologized for. Fort Worth would be a full night and half a day eastward. Soon they would cross dry East Fork. And north of that somewhere would be the old Ghost Ridge shack in the dense

19

mesquite thickets where Dock Tobin's band had hidden out that time after the Uvalde bank holdup. His mind flooded with the old memories. The robbery itself hadn't been half as terrifying to a seventeen-year-old kid as the long hole-up at Ghost Ridge. That was when Uncle Dock had likkered himself nasty-mean, argued over the loot, and drilled Buckshot Withers through the brain with a close-range .45 blast. Lincoln would never forget how Buckshot's bloody and ugly face still looked surprised, even after his body was cold as a slicker. His hatred for Uncle Dock had burned deeper than ever that night when Dock had made him bury Buckshot. That was when the reward posters were up in screaming black type all over the country, offering $1,000 dead or alive for any member of the Dock Tobin band. Including Dock's kid nephew, Link Jones.

CHAPTER TWO

The stop for wood at East Fork was, in the first few minutes, normal enough.

Two or three things stood out clearly in Lincoln's mind, later. The woman. The scattered cut wood for the engine, out north of the tracks. The man with the flat nose who came from the caboose end of the train.

The rest of it was always blurred.

First, as the train slowed, he saw the man coming down the aisle, a burly, pock-marked man, skin dark as a Mexican's, nose like a worn-out saddle horn. He had a scar across one side of his face that looked like a slice of bacon, and a dribble of black mustache. His wide-crowned hat topped a head pulled low to his wide chest, and his small black eyes whipped sidewise left and right as he moved down the shuddering coach.

The conductor bawled out, 'East Fork wood stop! All able-bodied men come give us a hand—more help we have, quicker we'll be on our way!'

The train slowed like a mule bracing on its haunches. Lincoln stood up, glad to stretch himself on stationary footing. He glanced dubiously at his valise on the overhead rack. Others seemed to be leaving their suitcases, though; he'd look funny trying to carry the thing and a load of wood at the same time. He supposed it would be all right left there.

Three or four men, joking good-naturedly about having to lug wood for the boiler, jostled down the aisle ahead of him and out the door. He followed, but at the vestibule his way was barred by Sam Beasley.

'Hell, let 'em go on, Jones! They'll never know whether we toted wood or not.' He winked wisely. 'You just watch Sam Beasley and I'll show you how to let them suckers do the dirty work. No use getting all sweated up

21

for the Fort Worth & Chihuahua.' He winked again.

'Happens I'd like a little exercise, Beasley. I don't mind carrying wood. You do what you want.'

'No, wait a minute,' Beasley insisted. 'Want you to meet a friend of mine. Coincidence, it is.'

The smell of the perfume again. The rustle of satin.

Lincoln knew she was just behind him and, turning, lifted his creased black hat.

She had reached the coach door, coming from behind them down the carpeted aisle.

The white feather tilted back. Her face turned up to him. He looked down into the engaging blue lights of her eyes. Blue that was lighter, not as solid as the steady blue of Lucy's eyes. But they caught on to him with a boldness he had not seen in a woman in a long time, not demure and not timid, with a smile at the back of them that seemed to say to a man that he would like what he saw.

'Billie Ellis,' said Beasley, flourishing cigar. 'Miss Billie Ellis. This here is Lincoln Jones. Friend of mine. From Odessa.'

'Hello, Odessa!'

Lincoln found her hand strong and pressing in his. It lingered there seconds longer than expected and he almost had to pull his own free after one pumping handshake. She had a nice friendly smile on her lips. Close up, her face

22

had a little more age and savvy behind it than he had expected. Age that the powder and paint did not quite conceal. Politely he said, 'Howdy-do, Miss Ellis.'

None of the hard-working calico-clad wives of the Odessa homesteaders, including Lucy, looked like this woman, even when they dressed up for a wedding or burying. She was small, but Lincoln estimated there was considerable figure to her beneath the dress-up train clothes and that if her harness had been cinched any tighter about the curves of hips and bosom, some inner gear would have ripped. Made everything seem extra noticeable, this close to her.

Beasley said, 'He's the most popular cattleman in the Odessa country.'

'Well, I don't know about that,' Lincoln said uncomfortably. 'I—'

'Don't be modest, Mr Jones.' Miss Ellis smiled. 'You know, I've always wanted to hear about that country out west. Why don't we all sit down while they're loading wood?'

Beasley examined his cigar as if he had just discovered it.

'Billie here is a schoolteacher,' he said. 'Out of a job.'

'Now, why would Mr Jones be interested in that, Sam?'

'Coincidence, it is, by gaddly,' Beasley said. 'He's looking for one.'

At that moment the door to the baggage car

23

opened and a man lounged there with a rifle carelessly under his arm. He lazily eyed the three in the vestibule and started to turn back, but stopped to squint again at Billie Ellis.

'Well, look what's with us! Where you headed for, Billie?'

She said shortly, '’Lo, Dave.'

'That crowd at the Longhorn get too rough for you?'

Miss Ellis's voice became coolly emphatic. 'You'd better go back to guarding the mail or whatever it is you're hired to do. Shoot yourself with that Winchester. And good riddance.'

Dave chuckled, waved a hand, and returned to the baggage car, slamming the door.

'I'd better get to lugging wood,' Lincoln said. He tried to edge past Beasley.

'That fellow must have got Billie mixed up with somebody else,' Beasley said.

'Doesn't matter!' Miss Ellis said gaily. 'Dave's the biggest rawhider in Crosscut.' She touched Lincoln's arm again and smiled. 'I'll watch all the big strong men carry wood.'

The first wood-loaded passengers were walking toward the engine from the mesquites. Lincoln passed them at a little distance, then headed at an angle toward the farthest scattering of cut green wood beneath a low rock outcropping. Soon he was alone in a bushy draw. He had simply walked away from Beasley and Miss Ellis, and now he was intent on stretching the kinks out of his cramped legs and getting his share of wood for the boiler. He kept on, heading for the most distant of the cut wood, wanting all the walking he could get to loosen his joints.

The first gunshot stopped one of his boot strides in mid-air.

He heard one shot, then three quick together, before he could turn around. A high yell sounded at the train. Horse hoofs rattled at a run, and a rifle cracked.

In a scrambling rush, he hurried back up the weedy rise, at the same time hearing high-pitched yells from near the rail embankment. At the top of the ridge he tripped headlong over a mesquite stump.

He hit hard, his breath leaving him with a whoosh. Dazedly he raised his head and looked toward the train. What he saw through the brush was a blur of confusion. There were men on rearing horses, blasts of gunfire, swirling dust, shouted curses.

He strained to see, to try to make some sense out of the dust-shrouded action. The men who had carried wood were now making a high run for the steps of the coach, fighting each other to get inside. Two riders with bandanna-covered faces wheeled back from the side door of the baggage car, twisting in their saddles, firing six-guns with wild aiming.

A third rider tore out of the brush. Dust boiled up. A rifle shot sounded again from the baggage car. Rock slivers splashed into Lincoln's face. Red sand rained down his neck, and sent him rolling back down the ridge. That wild bullet had been close.

From there he could see nothing. He was afraid to raise his chin from where he had buried it in dry grass. The shouts and noises faded.

Heavy footsteps pounded off to his left. Lincoln made a threshing turn on his stomach to see who this might be, and caught sight of a green suit fighting its way against the snagging clutches of mesquite thorns. Beasley, his breathing almost as loud as his feet, plunged out of the brush and plowed to the ground beside Lincoln. He lifted his fear-branded face to appeal for explanation.

'What is it, Jones? What're they doing?'

'Train holdup! You got a gun?'

'My God, don't mix in it!' Beasley's agonized look clung to Lincoln. 'Don't do anything! They might come shootin' at us.'

'Give me your gun, if you've got one!' Lincoln thought of his valise and felt sick. He had rather kill or be killed than to lose the Odessa money.

'It's just a little gun.' Beasley tried to squirm back from Lincoln. 'It wouldn't go any good.'

Lincoln caught him in a one-handed grasp, powerful enough to drag the frightened man close and tore into Beasley's coat pocket. He tugged out a short-nosed .32 nickel-plated revolver. Beasley pleaded, 'Don't shoot—let's just lay still and—'

Lincoln shoved Beasley aside and wormed to the top of the rise. He raised his head above the rock line, just in time to see the engineer scurry up the steps into the cab.

The engine whistle gave a short toot, steam hissed, and the stack spouted a cloud of smoke.

He could not find the mounted bandits through the mesquite growth, although a gun blasted from somewhere among the trees, toward the dry creek. An answering shot came from the baggage car. Somewhere he heard a running horse.

Lincoln suddenly unlimbered and sprang erect. He stared unbelieving. The truth sunk in. He saw the first turn of the wheels. The engine made the gasping struggle of starting up, and Lincoln yelled. With this movement in the bushes, a rifle barrel poked from the narrow opening of the baggage car door.

Lincoln called over his shoulder to Beasley. 'Come on—*run*! They're pulling out of here!'

Below the weedy slope Beasley moaned and staggered up.

'Don't let 'em leave us!'

'Hurry up—run!'

Beasley hopped upgrade like a wounded animal. 'I can't run—damn it, I got a bad sprained ankle.'

Lincoln saw then that Beasley was not going to make it. But he could run ahead and flag the engineer. Somebody would see him. Didn't the idiots know he and Beasley were not aboard?

He ran through the growth toward the tracks a hundred yards distant, waving his hand in the air, yelling. The rifle cracked again, a bullet whined past, and he felt a faint pluck at his left coat sleeve. This was followed by a mild stinging sensation in his upper arm.

Again, by instinct, he plowed to the ground and hugged it. *The damn fool was shooting at him.*

The rattle of the train onto the trestle drowned out the next shot but the bullet kicked dirt in his face.

When he dared raise his head, the end of the dinky caboose was leaping away in the distance and out of sight into the mesquite thickets around a curve on the other side of the bridge. He stumbled a few steps, then stood looking unbelievingly at the empty space, the gaping tracks. The last of the train's rattling flight noises thinned, faded, and died out. His ears were left only with a ringing silence, his brain churning in the enormity of the injustice in this. There went the valise, which was everything.

The whole thing was a crazy blur. It had happened in a few short minutes. And now the holdup men had disappeared, the train was gone—his money with it—and he was stranded afoot in empty country. With a panicky, crippled little fourflusher like Beasley.

Lincoln pulled his black felt hat off and

methodically brushed the red sand from it. The sun was hot, so he took his coat off, too. He fingered his shirt pocket for a tobacco sack. He saw the tear in his shirt sleeve and the pinkish stain where his arm was stinging.

That had been close. That rifle guard had been quick to pick any target he could see. Six inches to the right, and that bullet would have ripped his ribs instead of his sleeve.

Beasley came puffing up the incline.

'We got left.'

Lincoln looked down at the flabby man. He felt nothing but distaste for Beasley. But there was no use wrangling now about how he might have made the train if Beasley hadn't been on his hands. He guessed Beasley wasn't to blame for getting his ankle hurt.

'Yeah. We sure got left. How's your foot?'

'Can't hardly put weight on it. It's killing me.'

'Well, sit down and take the load off. We'll try to tie it up, because we've got a long ways to walk.'

Beasley sat down and looked around unhappily at the mesquite brush.

'I'm not goin' to be able to walk very fast—you won't go off and leave me, will you, Jones?'

'Not likely. Where would we walk to, anyhow?'

Beasley said hopefully, 'Maybe they'll back up and get us.'

'That engineer don't know we got left. He

won't stop till he runs out of wood or makes the next station, and that's a far piece. He stampeded. It was our lookout to get back on.'

Beasley mopped his face. 'A *holdup*—by gaddly, a holdup! That train must have been carrying bank money. That was why Dave Fletcher was riding guard.'

'Well, he sure whipped them off. He may not have hit one of them, but he fought 'em off and got away with his money.' Lincoln played absently with the cylinder of Beasley's gun, trying to think. Beasley began to unlace his high-topped shoe.

In the silence that followed, the approaching sounds behind them made both men whirl. Lincoln came up to a crouch with the revolver hammer cocked.

His shock at what emerged from the mesquites was almost as great as if the wild-riding bandits themselves had crashed from the brush.

Billie Ellis, her skirt held above dusty shoetops, and her perspiration-dampened hair straggling from beneath the hat, walked toward them.

The fetching look that Lincoln remembered was gone from the light-blue eyes, now set in hard displeasure.

'Did you see that fool engineer run off and leave us?' Miss Ellis demanded.

She halted before the two men, dropped her skirts, brushed angrily at the dust, and stared

30

accusingly from one to the other.

'Well, what are you going to do about it?'

'Nothing we can do, Miss Ellis. That train's just gone. That's all.'

She murmured a name with candid emphasis, for the engineer, a name Lincoln would not have suspected a schoolmarm of knowing.

'I agree with you heartily,' he said. 'But that's not getting us out of a fix. Your friend Beasley, here, has gone lame. Night's coming on.'

The mention of night caused both Billie and Beasley to look apprehensively over the empty ocean of mesquites. Beasley moaned. 'Won't be another train for three days, either way.'

Lincoln tried to put his mind to what they should do now. It was clear that these pale-faced city pilgrims would be of no help at anything, that whatever thinking was done he would have to do it himself. Without them on his hands, he would have started walking the crossties east until he came to something or somebody, if he had to walk all night. He frowned at the woman because she made a bad problem worse.

As Lincoln had already done, Billie Ellis removed her hat, gave a brush at the red dust settled on it, and tucked at the loose ends of her perspiration-dampened hair. The dark mass of it had a reddish tinge in the sunlight that Lincoln had not noticed on the train. Miss Ellis

31

looked unhappier than he and Beasley put together. Sparks of anger showed in her eyes, and a small tremble on her chin suggested that she might want to cry a tear but was too mad. Oblivious to both watching men, she slipped out of her suit coat. She punched the edges of her loosened shirt tails into her skirt waist, the stretching movements tightening the blouse fabric into intimate outlines that continued to roundly assert their full shapes even when she relaxed on a flat boulder. She looked hard at the men with lips firmed to a thin line and waited, as if it were up to them to bring the train back.

It was bad enough to be stranded with Beasley, and Beasley crippled. With the woman along, it was ten times worse. He studied her shoes. They wouldn't last two miles walking the tracks. Her eyes followed his inspection. She looked down, seeing that her ankles were exposed.

'Have you never seen a leg before?'

His ears turned hot. 'I was looking at your shoes.'

'Then the trip's worth it,' she said flatly. 'Men have been looking at me everywhere but my shoes since I was fifteen years old.'

'Right now,' said Lincoln, 'your shoes count for more than anything else you've got.'

'I never thought that the day would come.' Her blue glance smiled briefly, then she became serious again. Her face looked softer in repose, he thought, than when she was trying to use it for something. Come to think of it, he reckoned all women looked better that way, if they only knew it. Lucy was never prettier than when he saw her face relaxed in sleep.

Beasley said sullenly, 'How come you got left, too?'

She tossed her head and looked out over the empty country. 'A lady likes to take a walk sometimes. I was down there—' She motioned toward the gravel creek bed. 'I was just exploring, because the train was supposed to be here half an hour, somebody said. When all the excitement started, I hid behind the bank. And what big brave things were you doing, Sam Beasley? Dealing a few from the bottom of the deck?'

Beasley mumbled, 'Aw, shut up.'

Lincoln saw a squirming dark shadow in the broom weeds at the bottom of a huge mesquite bush a dozen paces to his right. He stooped, picked up a rock of fist size, and chunked it at the rattler, missing, but the small diamond-back slithered off in quick flight.

'How's the foot, Beasley?'

'It hurts. I need a drink. I ought to have a doctor. I might even have broke it. How we goin' to get out of here, Jones?'

'Mr Jones will carry you out, Sam,' Billie said scornfully. 'Or do you want me to piggy-back you to Fort Worth?'

'Don't be makin' fun of me, Billie, I'm

33

hurtin'.'

Lincoln could think of little but the Odessa money vanishing east with the train, of his carelessness, or so it now seemed to him, in not keeping the money strapped around him, even of his weakness in promising Lucy he would not wear his holster gun on the train. The trip he had anticipated with so much excitement had shattered about his head and he was losing patience with these two Crosscutters who were in nothing like the trouble he was in.

His long jawlines hardened, and both his seated companions tensed to the black look he fastened on them.

His anger at these two, at himself, at everything, died off as quickly as it had come over him. They couldn't help it, any more than he could. Now the thing to do was to get somewhere before the cold night set in. It was just another bad fix and he had been in one most of the time, one way or another, all his years. It was all anybody knew, in the Odessa country. Bad fixes to be got out of, somehow. Disconsolately, he moved his angular frame in a couple of steps aside to crush a slow-journeying tarantula under his boot.

'I think there's an old shack up the dry creek apiece,' Lincoln said, businesslike now in words and intentions. 'First thing we've got to do is find some shelter. You'd freeze out here tonight, Miss Ellis.'

'How far?' Beasley wanted to know.

But Billie Ellis, watching the tall man's face, showed a softening expression as she said shrewdly, 'He made you get left, didn't he? Could you have got to the train, if Sam hadn't been on your hands?'

'I don't know. Doesn't matter now. Every time I stuck my head up, that trigger-happy fellow in the baggage car was shooting at me. I guess he was locoed as the engineer, aiming at anything that moved.'

'Good heavens, you're hurt!'

'It's not much.' He wished these two were not along, that they didn't talk so much, that he could have a little silence to think in. Billie stood up and came over.

'Roll up your sleeve. Let me see that wound.'

Obediently he did so, and looked at the bloody streak across his arm just above his elbow. It wasn't bad, and he said so, but she set her lips firmly and insisted on tying her handkerchief around his arm.

'At least that will keep dirt out of the scratch. Now, Sam, let's see that ankle.'

She dropped to her knees before Beasley and felt the puffy flesh of his foot. Lincoln, watching, saw her white fingers explore Beasley's swollen ankle, and finally place it gently back on the ground. Beasley, eyeing her worriedly, asked, 'Is it bad, you think?'

'Can you hobble down to the creek? There's one little puddle of water down there—maybe if you soaked it a while it would help.'

'I doubt if I could get my shoe back on.'

'Well, good heavens, Sam, try! We can't just sit here a week while your foot's getting well.'

With Beasley hobbling slowly, they made it to the creek. Billie Ellis worked his shoe off again, and Beasley stuck his foot into a shallow hole of scummy water.

'Just where are we, anyhow?' Billie asked Lincoln. 'Do you know anything about this country?'

'A little. I was around here. Long time ago.'

Somewhere to the north would be Ghost Ridge. He wondered if somebody might be ranching there now. There might even be a ranch house, replacing the old adobe shack where they had holed up that time. Otherwise, as far as he knew, it was an empty country. A land of little grass, interminable mesquite thickets, worthless red ridges. Its barren miles reached for an eternity southward, nearly all the way to the Rio Grande. Northward, the mesquite finally gave way to the cap rock, and from there on, nothing but the bleak panhandle country.

He tried to put his mind back ten or eleven years. If he remembered right, Ghost Ridge house wouldn't be far to the north. It had been the shelter of some unknown nester who had tried his hand at running a longhorn herd in the mesquites, found it profitless, and had moved on. Others might have come and gone since.

He looked down the dry cut to where the

spindly-legged railroad trestle spanned two white chalk cliffs. The formation of those white banks looked familiar.

Was it his imagination? Or had he actually ridden along here in those days? Maybe he had come down to this very spot, from Ghost Ridge. By himself, or riding lookout with Claude Tobin. He remembered the hours of trying to hide from the others, of getting away from them, carrying in his young body his burden of resentment against them all, against the life that he had been plunged into when he had gone to live with Uncle Dock. Perhaps in those lonely days he had ridden here, a kid quick-made into a hard man, fearful and alert, sleepless from the chase, knowing the constant dread of the hunted.

On those rides, he remembered he had made his first uncertain plan to leave Uncle Dock. The yearning to escape had grown stronger and stronger, and he had had to pit his own crafty planning against the sharp-eyed crafty men with whom he lived. A gangling kid, then. Caught up in an alien world of violence. No close kin but the brutal man, almost a stranger to him, that they called 'Uncle Dock' and who was as much a terror to his own outlaw gang as he was to his kid nephew.

Lincoln remembered how he had finally come to the agonizing decision to cut loose and run. He had resolved that if he could get away from the Tobins he would go as far and fast westward as a horse could carry him. It had been a scheme hard to carry out. Uncle Dock was one who had seemed to read a man's mind right through his head. But Lincoln had learned, too. It had been a hard education, handed to him fast and rough; a world of guns and running horses and wild country and wilder men. It had taken weeks of thinking about, and the outfit had moved here and there, quickly and through the night. Skirmishes with the law on the one side, with Comanche war parties on the other, and often within their own group, in the edgy days of hiding, when idleness and whisky and arguments fed their angers, building into flare-ups of fist, knife, and even gunplay. He had grown from boy to man in a hurry, in those two years.

But Uncle Dock had controlled them. Not a man, not even Cousin Claude, but who feared Uncle Dock sober and who would no more have crossed him drunk than they'd have barehanded aggravated an old javali boar.

'Hey, you taking a nap?'

Her words pulled him back to the present. She was half reclining, a dozen feet away, sitting on her folded coat, her back to a rock. Her light-blue eyes were studying him, but they wavered when he locked his own direct gaze on her and she looked over at Beasley.

'Is it feeling any better, Sam?'

'I don't know,' Beasley grunted. 'Maybe a

38

little. By gaddly, this damn water smells worse than my foot.'

'A joke.' Billie looked at Lincoln and inclined her head toward Beasley. 'Sam's making a joke now, since all the shooting's over. I hate to mention it, but I'm hungry.'

She sat with her skirts ballooned modestly over her feet. Her head turned up to the afternoon sky, hands clasped about updrawn knees. Pretty profile the woman had. At a little distance, Lincoln thought, she looked younger than she probably was. Innocent-looking, which she probably wasn't, either. Schoolteacher looking for a job, was she? Lincoln grinned inwardly without humor. That was mighty pat. Even for Beasley. What did they think he was, a clodhopper from Odessa, ripe for plucking?

He'd like to see their expressions if he could tell them about the Sonora stagecoach job. Or of the burying of Buckshot Withers, when Uncle Dock had finally doubled up Buckshot's legs because Lincoln had dug the grave too short, and spaded dirt in on Buckshot half sitting up. Uncle Dock had patted down the last of the earth, ordered Lincoln to spread dead grass and brush on it, and had stalked back to the house and his bottle with the comment that if Buckshot didn't like the way he was sittin' he could figure out for himself how to lie down.

But Lincoln now tried to push that out of his

39

mind, the thoughts giving him no pleasure. But it was odd how it all came back this way, when he was in this country again. He had made his break that time. Link Jones had vanished into unknown land. The kid outlaw in Dock Tobin's rough outfit had been swallowed by a vast and untamed country. Now, on his first trip east in ten years, it was the life out *there* that strangely seemed unreal.

Billie Ellis spoke across to him. 'What are we going to do now, Mr Jones?'

'There's a shack somewhere north of here like I mentioned,' Lincoln said brusquely.

She nodded eagerly. 'Do you think we can find it?'

'We might. We can't sit here for three days until another train comes along.'

'Maybe they'll come back looking for us,' Beasley said, still hopeful.

'Maybe they will, and maybe not. But we don't know how long that will be, or whether they'll do it at all. I think we can get to that house, if you can hobble a few miles. We'd be better off there, than just sitting out here. It'll be cold tonight.'

Billie Ellis said, 'Do you suppose someone might be living at that place?'

'No telling. If we're lucky and there's a nester there, we might get horses. Can you get your shoe on, Beasley?'

He saw Beasley pull his foot from the water hole and reach for his sock and shoe. He saw

Billie Ellis extend a hand, and he took it, helping to pull her to her feet, seeing the fleeting smile of thanks in her eyes, and then she stooped to pick up her coat and hat. He turned back for his own coat, and when he did he saw the man standing above them, looking down from the low creek bank. He heard Billie Ellis's startled gasp and Beasley's mumble. He was the heavy scar-faced man Lincoln had seen on the train. He stood above them, with his mouth open and his arms dangling out.

He spoke to somebody out of sight over his shoulder. 'Here's what you saw movin', boys— c'mere and look.'

CHAPTER THREE

A shorter, younger, figure, heavy in the neck and shoulders, sky-lined himself on the ridge beside the other, and then a lanky older man joined the first two.

The younger one, with the long black sideburns of a Spanish dandy, said, 'Well, I be damn, three pilgrims got left afoot. Look at that filly, Ponch!'

'I'm lookin'. Maybe we ain't made a water haul after all.'

The three sets of eyes fixed on the woman. Lincoln heard Billie's fast breathing beside him. His first swell of elation at seeing any

41

human in this desolation now went hollow.

These were some of the train bandits. There was a danger here that he and Beasley would be helpless to do anything about, and the best to be hoped for was that the bandits would leave. He had been about to form words of explanation of their plight. These died unspoken. He waited, thinking of Beasley's gun inside his coat pocket.

The older one cursed impatiently. 'Let's get out of here. They ain't got anything on 'em.'

Scarface muttered audibly, 'I ain't thinkin' about money, Henny.'

Henny growled. 'We got that stuff to pick up and we ain't got all night. We already had trouble enough.'

He and the younger man vanished back from the creek ledge, and then Ponch walked out of sight, too. The three in the creek gravel stood unmoving for another minute. They heard the sound of horses die off somewhere in the mesquites. Lincoln mopped at the sweat beading his lips and glanced down at Billie. Her face was drained white.

*　　*　　*

Lincoln walked ahead.

His long legs felt no undue tiredness. There was no muscle about him that was a stranger to hard work and long hours of exertion. But his feet were burning like live coals in his high-

42

heeled boots. He had a horseman's aversion to travel afoot, hating to walk any distance at all when a horse could do the walking for him and a man could take his ease up in a good saddle where a man belonged. Sam Beasley and Billie Ellis wouldn't know how that was.

Those two limping behind him were town people. Beasley had the looks of a man who had never felt more sun than what stray streaks of it might have touched him, coming through the windowpane of a saloon gambling room. Miss Ellis, too, was not what he'd call somebody accustomed to outdoor discomforts. Especially not a walk through rough country. Not in those little thin shoes. Yet he had to admire the way she was taking this, uncomplaining. Her feet were probably killing her every step.

Well, none of them now looked anything like the same three people who had got on the train. If there ever was a bedraggled sight, Lincoln thought, it was the three of them with their clothes dirty and ripped, sweat-sodden, hungry, tired, and going nobody-knew-where, with the sun drifting down toward a night's rest the other side of El Paso.

The damn mesquites. Where nothing else in the Lord's unfinished land would grow, where no other seedling would dare to show one green blade in contest with the rocky ground and eternal drought, the thorny, worthless mesquites controlled the land. A horde of flourishing, needle-bristling parasites. From the cap-rock country in the north, and southward for three hundred lonesome miles nearly to the Rio, the mesquite thickets swept in a scrawny jungle, up the ridges and down the gullies. Cover for coyotes and rattlers and the roosting buzzards. But good for nothing else—a phony green dress that in summer could fool the Easterner into thinking it was a lush country, at first glance, until he got out in it afoot and saw the desolation. In the winter, as Lincoln well remembered, the whole land was a giant dead thing of black bare branches, suffering through its allotted time of sleet storms, cold, dark days, and nights of demon northers.

Walking like this, to a riding man, reduced him to the status of a clumsy ground creature, wobbling on his boot heels, stumbling over roots and rocks, toiling up eroded ridges and down across dry draws, forever going up and down, this way and that, to get around the mesquite clumps. Traveling the worst way and making no more than one mile for every two he had to walk, in such a twisting course.

Behind him, sometimes near, from the sounds of her footsteps, sometimes dropping far back, was Billie Ellis. And struggling along, back of Billie, was Sam Beasley.

Lincoln decided it was time for a short rest again, for if it was hard going for him, it must be doubly mean for those two. He picked a place on the edge of a shallow gully and sat.

Watching for the woman, he saw her emerge from the last mesquite thicket, peering ahead anxiously as if afraid she had lost him. She carried her suit jacket folded over her arm, with the same hand clutching the little hat, as if they were treasures to cling to at all costs. The disarray of her outlining blouse, the loose strings of dark hair that had escaped the pins, the thorn snags in her skirt, were matters she seemed resigned to, as if they were unimportant one way or another.

'We'll rest a minute,' he said, 'and let Beasley catch up.'

When she dropped to the thin dry grass not far from him, she appeared too tired to care whether her action was graceful, or what momentary exposure of white petticoat and torn stocking her movements created.

She relaxed, trying to find comfort on the ground. He saw the escaped fullness within her blouse as she turned on her side, facing him, her head supported on one elbow. With one hand she absently smoothed down her skirt. She pushed toe against heel, one then the other, working off her shoes.

'You'll have a hard time getting them back on,' he warned.

'I don't care. I don't care what happens. I just want to rest.'

He got up and walked over to her. He stopped, extending his folded coat.

45

'Put this under your head. Watch out for red ants in a few minutes. They'll find you.'

He went back to where he had been sitting and listened for Beasley.

In a moment she spoke drowsily.

'Thanks for the coat.'

'If Beasley's gun's in the way, in the pocket, just shift it around. No, I'll take it.' He got up and went back, located the gun when she raised her head, and worked it into his pants under his belt.

She said, 'This is wonderful, just to rest. A bed would be better, though.'

Because he was facing her, he had to see how she wiggled her stockinged toes as she lay back and crooked her arm across her face, her hair loosely massed upon his coat. Such a thing as only a woman could do, the way that only a woman could look in doing it, rubbing her tired stockinged feet against each other that way, trying to push some of the burn out of them. He tried to put on the same unconcern between them in this small thing of intimacy. But he couldn't help seeing that her legs were trim and prettily shaped. He had strange knowledge of the feminine nearness of her, aware that he was long unaccustomed to seeing any woman beside Lucy in anything but the most rigid regard for concealing modesty.

'My suitcase!' Miss Ellis said vehemently. 'All my clothes! I hope that engineer fries in Hades for this.'

46

'We'll get our things back,' Lincoln said with more confidence than he felt. 'Guess the railroad will have them for us when we get to Fort Worth.'

He wasn't so sure. He might never see that six hundred dollars again. If it was lost he'd have to work years to pay back his neighbors, and he would always be the laughingstock of the country.

'When we get to Fort Worth!' she repeated glumly. 'If ever.'

Beasley hobbled up, puffing. He saw them resting and tossed his coat to the ground where he was and sprawled on it.

'How much farther's that place, Jones?'

'Can't tell how far we've traveled, the way we've been circling through this brush.'

'I saw a rattlesnake back there. I don't like this damn country.'

'I've seen four,' Lincoln replied. 'It always had more rattlers than anything else.'

'Why didn't you kill them?' Miss Ellis demanded.

'Killing four wouldn't make a bit of difference in the population. If we stopped for that we'd be here a year.'

'That damned engineer!' Beasley jabbed a new cigar in his mouth and slapped his clothes for a match. 'Not only left us—he went off with everything I own.'

'Marked decks and all, I guess,' Miss Ellis said.

47

'We'll get our stuff back,' Beasley said viciously, 'or we'll sue the Fort Worth & Chihuahua to its last crosstie. Wait'll I get to a telegraph station somewhere. I'll burn up the wires. I guess you had your schoolteacher money in your valise, didn't you, Jones? Or do you carry it on you?'

'Oh, forget the whole thing, Sam,' Miss Ellis said wearily.

'Money was in the valise,' Lincoln said.

'What was it all about?' Miss Ellis wanted to know.

He told her. He made it brief, not wanting to sound braggy; how the Odessa people, all the homesteaders and the families scattered for miles on their hard-grubbing little cattle spreads, had hoped to bring a teacher into the far-distant frontier country, so that their children could have schooling. Longhorns were plentiful out there, but cash dollars were scarce. It had been no easy thing, to dig up six hundred dollars. And they had selected Lincoln Jones to make the trip to Fort Worth to try to hire a teacher.

Miss Ellis listened without comment, one arm resting across her eyes, her head pillowed on his coat.

Lincoln said, 'When the train left, so did the money.'

'And there went a good idea, Sam,' Miss Ellis said sharply.

'This has sure ruined my trip.' Beasley

48

groaned.

Lincoln laughed shortly. It was too bad about Beasley.

'Your trip was ruined when Marshal Kincaid first suggested that you pack and take the next train out of Crosscut,' Miss Ellis remarked.

'Crosscut's a stinkin' damn place, anyway,' Beasley said. 'Be glad to get out of there and back to Fort Worth. Gaddly, this ankle's a sight! Jones, don't you have any idea where that place is? Seems to me we've walked ten miles.'

Lincoln was thinking about the valise. He had troubled visions of the bag being confiscated by some thieving passenger, or winding up lost in the mysterious inner workings of the railroad headquarters, wherever that was.

How would it sound, if he finally had to go home, broke and no teacher, saying he'd lost the money? Lost it his very first day on the train! Some of them would never believe him. They'd hound him out of the country, make Lucy and the kids a laughingstock, disgraced for life. It was a tormenting thought. Grimly, he argued back to himself that he'd get that money if it took a year. That was a dead certainty.

But first things had to come first. They had to get out of here, make their way out of this empty country and to the next station east.

Might be fifty miles to Eskota. Wherever it was, it would have a telegraph station, and like Beasley said, they could start the railroad to finding his valise.

Beasley spoke across to them in a bleak, faraway voice. 'You know what I think? I don't like the looks of this. I feel like maybe I'll *never* see Fort Worth again.'

'Fine talk,' Billie Ellis scoffed. 'Get a little starch in that backbone, Sam.'

'I got a strong intuition.'

'A blackjack intuition? Feel like you've dealt yourself a bust?'

'I don't know what it is.' The jumpy eyes in the pie-dough face flitted unhappily back and forth across the sweeps of the mesquite roughs. 'Just got a crawly feeling.'

'It's your ankle,' she said. 'You'll be all fired up again, Sam, once you get a Fort Worth beefsteak under your belt and a card table in front of you and a deck in your hands.'

Billie Ellis shifted her body and looked at Lincoln.

'What about you, Odessa? You got any intuitions under that hard, solemn Indian expression of yours?'

'Usually I just cross the creeks one at a time,' said Lincoln.

'I'll bet you sure as the devil cross 'em when you do come to 'em,' she commented, studying him. 'You got that Gentleman from Odessa look that would make a creek run uphill to get

50

out of your way, I imagine, if you happened to come on it a little riled up.'

It wasn't any of his business, he thought, how these two looked at things. They were a different tribe from him and the quicker he got away from them the better it would suit him. Circumstances had thrown them together in an unlucky situation, and he felt he had to help them get out of the mess. But he had seen their kind before, in the old days. Out of their element, like this, they were about as helpless as a cottontail in a coyote pack. Beasley was on the verge of panic, looked like; and the woman was talking a lot braver than she felt.

'You two don't want to be hollering before you're hurt,' he said, intending to buck them up a little. 'Maybe this walking's bad, maybe our plans have been jumbled up a trifle, each one of us in his own way.'

'Oh no,' Billie said lightly, 'this is a perfectly love-ly picnic.'

'Well, I never did see a longhorn bogged so bad in quicksand he couldn't be pulled out, one manner or another. Now, after while we'll find that house I know about. If anybody lives there, we'll get food and we'll have transportation pretty quick to the next place on the railroad. If they don't, we'll at least have shelter for the night, and we'll rustle some food some way, and eventually somebody will find us. So about all we got to worry about now, actually, is our feet.' He gave the girl a one-sided grin. 'I reckon the Lord wouldn't have given them to you to ache occasionally if He hadn't invented stirrups, too, so you would appreciate how good it is to get off of 'em. Well, a lot of things are like that.'

'That's quite a speech,' Billie said after a moment.

Beasley groaned, chewed his cigar, and rubbed his ankle. 'Prayer meetin' ain't gettin' us out of here.'

Lincoln pulled out a tobacco sack. 'You look at it your way, and I'll look at it mine.'

Billie Ellis came up to an elbow and Lincoln was surprised to sight a luminous moistness in the blue eyes. 'I agree with what you said—Lincoln,' she said quietly.

He worked at the smoke, looking at his fingers. 'It's all right—Billie.'

He ran the cigarette across his lip, crimped the end, felt for a match. 'You think you can manage another mile or two, now? Sun's getting low.'

'I think I can. How about you, Sam?'

'Can't we rest a minute longer?' Sam demanded. 'I just got here. You two ain't got a busted ankle like I got. Jones, you got another match?'

Lincoln went over and handed a match to Beasley who made a sign to Lincoln before firing the cigar. Beasley lowered his voice.

'What about those men? You think they're gone for good? I didn't like the looks of them,

Jones!'

'Bandits never are appetizing to look at. Especially after they'd got fought off their baggage-car holdup like that.'

'But do you think they're gone?' Beasley insisted.

'Yes. Getting gone from here is the thing they'd want the most. If we were going to have any ruckus with them, it would have been back there when they spotted us. They got no more use for us than we got for them.'

'I sure didn't like the looks of them,' Beasley repeated. 'The way they stood up there, taking us in.'

His voice carried to the woman.

'They weren't eyeing *you*, Sam,' she called.

Lincoln went back to sit again while Beasley was having his smoke. Billie said, 'I was scared back there, for a minute. No use denying it.'

He could have told her that he had been alarmed, too. Not about himself, or Beasley. But in the way the man with the scarred face was looking at Billie.

'What I can't understand,' Beasley said now, puffing smoke, 'is why they came back at all. Why didn't they strike out after the shootin' and keep moving? The train was gone. Been me, I'd a lit a shuck far as a horse would run.'

'That's puzzled me, too,' Lincoln admitted. 'Anyhow, Beasley, they're gone. Their holdup failed, and they'll be doing just what you said—riding far and fast before the hunt can

53

get organized and started.'

'Don't know who would hunt them anyhow. No towns anywhere along here. Nothing between Crosscut and Eskota—hundred miles of nothing. Don't see some deputy sheriff wantin' to spend two or three days ridin' by hisself out here, not knowing what he's ridin' after in the first place, the trail old and cold.'

Lincoln stood up. 'Let's get a move on.'

They started out again, but this time Lincoln slowed his gait, enabling Billie to keep up with him. Beasley hobbled a distance behind.

'That youngest man,' she said, 'the heavy one who called us the three pilgrims. I've seen him before, Lincoln. I just know I have. Those fancy sideburns, the way he looked so proud of himself.'

'Where do you think you've seen him?'

'I don't know. Laredo. Or Angelo, maybe. Maybe Crosscut. It could have been right there in the Longhorn Palace.'

'You worked there, did you?'

She flashed a puzzled glance up at him. 'Didn't you know?'

'I thought,' he said dryly, 'you were a schoolteacher. Looking for a job.'

'Oh, *that!*' She made an impatient motion, as if this was of no consequence. 'That was just Sam's idea.'

'You were going to pretend to be a schoolteacher. And Sam was going to figure a way to fleece me. Was that it?'

54

'Something like that,' she said, nodding. Her eyes sought his face, worriedly. 'He didn't take time to explain everything to me. I don't know what he had in mind. I don't usually do things like that, Lincoln, honest. But I was willing to make some money.'

'What did you do at the Longhorn?'

She smiled, as if this question amused her. 'Good heavens, Lincoln—where have you been so long? I was the singer there. Didn't you ever hear of the Girl with the Golden Voice? That's the way the Longhorn advertised me.'

'I never was around Crosscut,' Lincoln said. 'I think that's right nice. Singing.'

She made a grimace. 'The singing was all right. But you don't know what it is to have a rough crowd of men out there at the bar, staring at you, night after night, undressing—' Her voice broke off.

'Undressing?'

'With their eyes. You know how I mean. But it's always like that. One place is about like another. The piano player's just harder to fight off in some.'

'But you would have changed from a singer to a little fleecin' job, you and Sam. If you thought there'd be money in it. Off of a greenhorn from Odessa, like me. Is that what you were going to do?'

Impulsively, she touched his arm, plodding on with him through the roughs. 'Yes, I suppose so.' She looked up, eyes honest and

55

unwavering. 'I was going to take you in, Lincoln. Any way I could.'

CHAPTER FOUR

The old man in the rocker was facing the fireplace in the Ghost Ridge house.

The chair tipped slowly, back and forth, squeaking and complaining beneath the two hundred pounds of muscular bulk, throttled on its arms by the grip of two enormous hands. The man's huge head, with its tangle of rusty gray hair, was held erect, in an attitude of constant listening. His eyes never batted, the film over the staring black pupils reflecting no color from the yellow flames. The fire raced fugitive shadows in unending flight around the dim, bare room, as if they tried to escape the moaning sounds of human suffering that came regularly from the adjoining bedroom.

The old man might have been of any age between sixty and eighty. He still had powerful size, though age had slacked his skin loosely and all his large features appeared to sag, as if their weight had finally broken down the hide that held them. Only his mouth was undersize, a stringy knife slice of an opening, lipless almost, and all but lost in the unshaved crop of gray stubble that covered his face like frosty cactus.

A rumble began in the caverns of his chest beneath a black vest caked with old food drippings, worked up through the collar of his brown flannel shirt, and thundered out the knife slit.

'Coaley! Come here, Coaley!'

The burlap-sack curtain was pulled aside back of him, where the timbered kitchen lean-to hooked on to the 'dobe room. A stooped man with buzzard-beaked nose peered in. He carried two six-guns on his legs and a skillet in his hand.

He answered in a surly voice. 'What'd you want?'

'Coaley! Where's Coaley?'

'Coaley's outside. You sent him out to look around. Quit botherin' me now, if you want any supper.'

The curtain dropped.

The big man in the chair continued to rock and stare unblinkingly at the fire. His chest rumbled again.

'Alcutt in there—I'm tired of him taking on.'

The answering voice from the kitchen was gruffly patient. 'Well, I don't see why he can't take on if he wants to. It's his house and it's his belly that's got a bullet in it.'

The old man rocked on, as if the conversation had never taken place.

The low moaning of a man in torture came at unvarying intervals from the other room.

The outside door opened and a heavy-set,

57

swarthy man came in from the night. His boots clomped loudly on the bare floor. The flickering firelight touched the burned-bacon scar across his cheek, giving it red edges and accenting the doughy bulk of a shapeless nose.

The old man, without turning his head, said, 'Everything all right out there?'

'*Si.* Coaley, he watch.'

'Ponch—whose fault was it?'

The swarthy one sank to a bench against the wall. His voice was an uneasy grumble. 'Like I told you, it just happened bad. *Bad.*'

'Damn you, I know that.'

'Nobody's fault, honest. That guard with the rifle—It was his fault mostly.'

'You think there was a tip-off, Ponch?'

'No. That guard—he just started shooting. Alcutt got shot off his horse. All of us, we nearly got killed. Lucky we ain't like Alcutt.' He looked toward the darkened bedroom where the groans kept coming.

'Wait till Claude gets back,' the old man mumbled. 'He'll know what went on at the Crosscut end. You get the stuff off the coach?'

'*Si.* We been back for it. It was in the weeds where I threw it out the window. It's all out there in the barn. We ain't looked it over yet.'

The old man kept sitting with his head erect, facing the fire.

'Maybe you could have got off the train sooner. You scared to get out there?'

Ponch protested with an obscenity. 'I done

58

just like I was supposed to do. Ask Coaley or Henny. Soon as everybody was off the coach, I started throwing the valises out the window on the far side, down the bank, so we could pick 'em up later. Then I tried to get the door open at the end of that baggage coach, but the fellow had locked it tight. So I got off on the other side, where Henny had left me a horse. Time I rode around the train to where Henny and Coaley and Alcutt was, there was shootin' like you never saw. We was damn lucky. Luckier'n this fellow Alcutt in there.'

'He didn't want to go in the first place. If he don't shut up that taking on, I'll give him something to take on about. He's been whinin' ever since we hit here.'

'Well, this was his place,' Ponch muttered. That was what the man in the kitchen had said. For the first time, the big head turned, the rocker stopped.

'I'm gettin' sick of you, Ponch Izaguirre. I wish to God I was able to run my own deal again.'

'I wish to God I was back in Saltillo,' Ponch growled. 'Without havin' to ride there, with maybe half of Texas huntin' us.'

'Thinking of running out on me, Ponch?'

'Nosir, *nosir*! Not thinking nothing like that!'

'Ponch, you ain't got any guts. One of these days I'm goin' to cut you open and prove it. Or get Coaley to do it—Coaley would take you down and show me what was inside that big belly of yours, if I told him to. Coaley—'

'You just ask me to do something!' Ponch stoutly protested. 'I got as much guts as Coaley or anybody. You never tried me out. You always let Claude boss things.'

'I'll try you out.'

The old man's chuckle was like a sick cough. He stood up, his head swinging over the room, as if seeking Ponch. His staring eyes fixed finally on the scarred face. Ponch nibbled at his straggly mustache, his fat hands clutching the edge of the bench.

'You go in there and stop that fellow from moanin' all night. You go do that, Ponch, if you got so much guts.'

'Stop him?' Ponch breathed. 'How am I gonna stop him?'

'You got a gun.'

'You mean—'

'Stop him any damn way you want to—just so you stop that noise.'

'God—I ain't gonna—'

'No guts!' The two words tore out in a snarl.

Taking one deliberate step after another, his head held rigidly high, the old man moved his great bulk in ponderous motion into the bedroom.

Ponch closed his eyes, his head back against the wall, big knuckles white where he gripped the bench. The beaked-nose man in the kitchen stopped the clattering of pans and came to the

60

burlap curtain, pulling it open a crack. He looked at Ponch, then at the back of the man walking into the gloom of the bedroom.

Ponch groaned. 'Henny, stop him!'

Henny only stood there, his hand frozen where he held the burlap.

Henny and Ponch seemed to quit breathing. The blast of the gun shook the house. The acrid smell of burned powder drifted out of the room. The shadows danced on the wall. Ponch opened his eyes. Henny dropped the curtain. The sound of pans on stove top resumed. The old man came back in his measured stride, his right hand slipping a .45 into his hip holster. He stalked to the chair. The rocking started up again. The old man made a chest rumble. The moaning in the bedroom had stopped.

'You got no guts, Ponch. Never knew a greaser that had any guts.'

The door opened and from outside, where the dusk was deepening into first darkness, came rapidly an overmuscled, stocky youth whose fist nursed the gun butt in his leg holster. He had smooth olive skin, fuzzy on the plump cheek lines, black eyes crowded together, and long black hair greased down.

He looked quickly from the old man to Ponch. 'What was that shootin'?'

Ponch only stared down at the floor.

'What was it?' the young man repeated. 'I heard a shot in here.'

'Calm down, Coaley.' The old man kept

61

rocking, not turning his head. 'That feller in there, the one that got wounded at the train. He was going to die anyway. No use to sit here and let a man bleed to death.'

Coaley released his grip on the Colt butt. After a moment he walked across the room with a loose-hipped swagger. His head with its long black sideburns cocked at a challenging tilt, his bull-heavy shoulders swinging. He parted the folds of an embroidered suede jacket and thrust a hand carelessly into the right pocket of his tight-fitting yellow corduroys. His white-stitched yellow boots carried him importantly wherever he walked. He went to the bedroom, and in there the boots stopped for a moment, as if even their badge of self-assurance had been challenged.

When Coaley came back he reached his hand in a studied move and parted the curtain to the kitchen, leaning a shoulder against the doorframe.

'What we got to eat, Henny?'

Henny didn't bother to answer.

The old man in the rocker laughed hoarsely.

'You're a great one, Coaley!'

Coaley nodded, pleased. It was now established that Coaley Scull was a man of hard guts, not squeamish, not a man to have his appetite blunted by any bloody mess. He tilted a superior glance down to Ponch, and walked to the fireplace, his heavy weight shifting in careless sway from one boot to

62

another, his plump right hand twirling a plaited-leather watch string.

'We got a lot of stuff out in the barn. All those suitcases sagged both pack horses. Mostly clothes. You need a few new petticoats, a camisole or two, any long-handled drawers good as new?'

But the old man showed annoyance and the smile went off Coaley. 'We got a little money, too. One of them valises had six hundred dollars in it.'

'Six hundred! We stood to get twenty thousand!'

Coaley shrugged, standing spraddle-legged before the fire. 'We just had hard luck.'

The old man hammered a rocker arm. 'I'd like to know where the slip-up was! There was twenty thousand dollars in that baggage car. It's took me three months to plan this one and it's cost a hell of a lot of money to work it out, moving up here and all, and we're a hell of a long way from the border. I do everything, plumb bust a gut to work this one up right, sending Claude to Crosscut, putting Ponch on that train so he can signal to you at the wood stop if the money's on it, work it out how we're going to get back to Nuevo Laredo with our scalps, and then you-all come draggin' tail in with *nothing!* One man shot in the belly, no loot, and you talking about six hundred dollars!' He spat loudly toward the fire, causing Coaley to jump.

'Claude will know what happened,' the old one grumbled. 'Wait'll he gets back from Crosscut. He ain't gonna like this.'

Coaley's finger skipped a swing of the plaited leather. 'Claude ought to have been with us today,' he murmured.

'No, I wanted him in the town, to see which way the chase starts. We needed to know that.'

'I'd like to of seen him out there, nothing to shoot at but a crack in a door, and a guy sending thirty-thirty bullets like he knew how. The Crosscut end of this deal was pretty easy.'

'You mouth too much, boy.'

Ponch fed words to the old man, making his tone admiring. 'You planned it mighty smart, you sure did, and this ain't the only job. Next time we'll haul off a wagonload of money.'

Coaley went to the door, taking his time. There he paused and looked across at Ponch.

'You gonna take your turn at lookout tonight—or just sit there like a potbellied stove with the fire out?'

Ponch mumbled, showing yellow teeth in a snarl at Coaley. 'How come you went through those suitcases at the barn? What was your hurry?'

Henny drawled from beyond the kitchen curtain, 'He wanted to feel of them petticoats. So he'd know what they was when he gets old enough to encounter 'em.' Henny cackled.

'I'll cut your throat, Henny.'

Henny struck the curtains apart. He flung a

64

short, hard word at the youth. 'Just start tryin' it any damn time you're ready.'

'When I do you'll know it.'

The old man spoke. 'You bury Alcutt, Coaley.'

'Me bury him? Hell—*why me?*'

Ponch made a laugh die in his throat.

The old man locked his fingers across his chest and rocked. Coaley straddled a rawhide chair across from the rocker, and made conversation, telling it again, how the holdup went. Ponch, dozing, opened his eyes a slit once and mumbled, 'You ain't gonna talk him out of it, Coaley.' But Coaley kept on.

Ten minutes had passed, with the old man doing little more than occasionally grunting in response to Coaley's rambling talk, when the footstep sound came to them from outside the door.

The old man stiffened and stopped rocking, his hand going to the six-gun.

Coaley shot across the room, jerking open the door.

Lincoln saw Coaley first, then Ponch, in the gloom. Both of them had guns in their hands, both stood stiff, confronting him. He had no time to glance at the figure half shielded by the high-backed rocking chair.

The old Ghost Ridge place, looming up in the darkness, had looked good to him, until this moment. There had been wagons and horses at the pen, smoke curling from the

65

chimney, ample signs that the old place was inhabited. He had confidently expected that whatever struggling nester was working it would have shelter, food, and mounts to offer the three fagged-out strangers. The thought of these things, of their luck at finding help in that desolation, had overwhelmed his bad taste for the place, the deep-seated uneasiness that always came with any thought of Ghost Ridge. The ridge itself, a low, sharp-edged rock line, bare of any trees at all, jutted up like half-buried skeleton fingers a mile to the north, a dark trademark to his bad times here.

The opening of the door produced a shock as jolting as a tomahawk on the head. What he saw then left him naked of any comprehension except the big sickening one that he had made a terrible mistake.

Two sets of unfriendly eyes, like the black holes in the gun muzzles trained on him, held him stiff in his tracks, halfway into the room.

'Come on inside!' Coaley invited.

Lincoln closed the door behind him, watching the two with the guns.

Flickering light from the fireplace was enough to show flecks and flashes of the features he remembered back at the dry creek. The train bandits.

He stood voiceless and sweaty. His ears rang with the fact before him. This was a bad thing.

Ghost Ridge was a robbers' hole-up place again and he had walked straight into it. Worse

66

than that, he had brought Beasley and Billie with him.

Coaley enjoyed the openmouthed surprise in the visitor. He worked the six-gun muzzle tauntingly back and forth.

Lincoln thought, *It's a thing I'll have to go at mighty careful—All I want is to get out of here.*

He forced the confusion to subside in his mind by putting on a tight grin of his own, right back at Coaley.

'Looks like I called at the wrong time.'

'It's one of the passengers.' Coaley spoke over his shoulder. 'One of the three pilgrims we saw in the dry creek. They got left.'

There was a grunt at the rocking chair.

'I was looking for a roof for the night,' Lincoln said. 'But maybe you'd be better satisfied if I just moved on—I can manage all right in the open. All right with you if I get along now?'

He waited, looking from Coaley to Ponch, at their guns, and now, in the kitchen doorway, at Henny.

Ponch growled warningly to Coaley. 'He ain't no ordinary pilgrim. Watch him! Where you hail from, mister?'

'Why, I'm from out at Odessa,' Lincoln said matter-of-factly, 'I was on the train, headed for Fort Worth, and—'

'Gentleman from Odessa,' Coaley leered. Ponch chuckled deeply.

Coaley said, 'I always wanted to see what a

67

live one looked like.'

Henny said, 'And, by God, he looks it.'

'You that tough?' Coaley prodded. 'Ponch, what you think?'

Ponch muttered, 'I don't like nothing about this.'

In the following long moment of silence, broken at first only by the sputter of the firewood and the first small whistle of the night breeze through the wall cracks, the old man's voice cut heavily across the room.

Without turning his head, almost as if he spoke from his sleep, he said, 'Come on in, Link. Come over here where I can see you. Come shake hands with your Uncle Dock Tobin.'

CHAPTER FIVE

Lincoln felt the voice cut into his brain from out of the past, ripping the years away.

And the past became the present, blurred and mixed, overflowing into one span of time. It was crazily as if he had never been anywhere but here at Ghost Ridge, that he had only stepped out of the room a little while.

Now, as then, his uncle's words compelled his legs to move. Unbelieving, yet knowing it was so, he stared at the man in the chair. He walked woodenly past Coaley, across to the

68

fireplace, to the side of the rocker.

Uncle Dock hoisted himself up towering to his feet and turned his head to search for Lincoln's face.

'You've growed.'

He extended a hand, then, and Lincoln shook with him.

'Hello, Uncle Dock. Didn't expect to find you still here.'

Confusedly, he had the tangled thought that Uncle Dock must have been right here all the ten years.

'I don't see good, any more. But I'm sensitive in my hearing. I knew that was you, Link, the minute I heard you talk.' He peered up close to Lincoln's face, as if trying hard to pierce a fog that retarded his vision. 'You look just the same. Only older.'

Uncle Dock added, 'You been gone a spell. When did you get back, boy?'

Puzzledly, Lincoln looked away from him, throwing a questioning glance to the other men. But neither showed change in set faces. They stood where they had been, six-guns still in their hands, although their gun arms hung down, now, and the black muzzle holes were no longer on him.

'I just got back,' Lincoln said numbly. 'Got left by that train down there today.' Then he added, because his brain was working again and he knew he was in a tight spot, 'Your boys had a little tough luck, I reckon. Had a little

69

myself—got shot in the arm by that sharpshooter in the baggage car.'

The old man said, 'You run off and left me.'

'Yeah, wanted to strike out west a ways. Sort of look around. You know how a fellow gets itchy feet.'

Uncle Dock sat down in the chair, adjusted the six-gun around to his lap, and folded his fingers over it.

'I don't like for my kin to leave me. We all belong together. I needed you, boy. These others—they ain't no good.' He said that in gruff contempt, as if not caring that the three stood listening. His voice made another of its abrupt tone changes, and he said, 'Except Coaley—he's all right. Coaley and Claude. They're your cousins, Link. Second cousins, I reckon it is. That's Coaley there by the door.'

Lincoln gave Coaley a studying look. Coaley was about twenty-one and too proud of himself. Too big in the head and shoulders and all over. Sideburns too fancy. He could see the wash of yellow flecks in his eyes, the color of weakness and coyote cunning.

Lincoln said, 'Claude? Claude Tobin? Is he here?'

'He'll be here.' Uncle Dock raised his head and searched for Lincoln. 'Then I'll have three of my own kin with me. You and Claude and Coaley. I got some big plans, Link. I wish you hadn't been gone so long.'

'You always had some big plans, Uncle

Dock. But this time, I can't stay. I got to keep moving.'

'What's the matter, boy? Law after you?'

'Nothing serious, I just need to keep moving.'

'Well, you can move right along with us. Talk about moving—we're fixed up for the damndest move you ever heard of. It's a way we figured up, to get back out of this country and down to Nuevo Laredo, after the holdup. No, *you* tell him about it, Coaley.'

Coaley rocked on his boots. 'Uncle Dock's a little weak in the eyes. Can't ride a horse, at least not in a hurry, over rough country. The way we were going to skip south, was in two covered wagons. Rigged up like an immigrant outfit. Travel at night, hole up in the day. Even if a law did spot us at a distance, who'd figure a crowd of train robbers ploddin' along in covered wagons like ignorant nesters?' Coaley swung back and forth on his feet, and began twirling the plaited string.

Ponch put in, 'And you know who thought of that?' He nodded at the chair. 'Your Uncle Dock, of course.'

'Of course,' Coaley echoed.

'We'll get you out of the country,' Uncle Dock said reassuringly. 'You got here at the right time, Link. We'll have a little drink around and eat some supper. Henny! *Henny Lake!* Bring that bottle in here!'

Coaley had his hand on the doorknob, but

71

instead of opening the door he pressed his ear against it. He signaled to Ponch, then whispered across to Uncle Dock. 'Be quiet! Somebody talking out there!'

Lincoln stalked to the door. Coaley moved aside, looking at him with narrowed eyes.

'They're with me. The two who got left by the train.'

Uncle Dock was on his feet. 'I don't like strangers.'

A grin broke out on Coaley. 'Oh, the filly. Is *she* out there?'

'There's a lady out there. And a man. The train got away from us. We hiked up here afoot.'

Ponch slouched forward. 'The girl. *Ah!* So the holdup was not such a bad water haul after all.'

Coaley made a smacking sound. 'I'll say it wasn't!'

'You ain't old enough,' Henny commented.

'What you think!' Coaley retorted. 'Better'n being too godderned old.'

'Me, I bring'em in.' Ponch started for the door.

Lincoln barred his way.

This had to be it. The situation stood before him, stripped of trimmings like the bare walls of the room.

These would be the only caliber of men that would work with Uncle Dock. Strangers to all normal decencies, selfmade badmen, careless

72

killers.

The smirk on Coaley, the words of Ponch. Lincoln saw its shaky balance, and knew that whatever tilting he did to his predicament, one way or the other, had to be done now, in this moment. Somebody had to get top hand here before the girl came into the room. Them or him. Whatever bad blood had been in him at birth, he had worked ten years to get the stain out. Now, it stirred again and he felt the years slip back. He was among his own. The knowledge came and the decision wrote itself in the silence. *From now on he had to be one of them.* It was the only way of saving his own life, likely, and Beasley's; and the life, or something more, or less, according to how she looked at it, of Billie Ellis.

He had to be Dock Tobin's returned nephew. The outlaw who had ridden as Link Jones in the old days with Uncle Dock's bad ones. And as that direction opened to him, he saw quickly he would have to force the gamble that, for a little while at least, he would get the backing of the old man at the fireplace. Otherwise, there would be three murders done here without the bat of an eye, for he and Billie and Beasley knew the identities of the train bandits.

They waited. Lincoln looked from one to another, making a slow, eye-squinting, plainly unimpressed tally of these, his uncle's latest hired hands.

73

Coyotes didn't snap their fangs at another coyote if the other one was strong and sharp-fanged, himself. They jumped only on the cripples.

He began with Henny, letting the other two dangle. But he made a long silence hang there, between the time he fastened a significant stare on Henny and the time he fed the words out like Henny was a little thickheaded and had to hear a simple thing twice.

'Uncle Dock told you to bring in the whisky, friend.'

Uncle Dock mumbled, 'By God, I sure did, Henny.'

Henny disappeared into the kitchen.

The saddle stoop came out of Lincoln's shoulders. He locked a gaze on Coaley, so hard that Coaley's smirk died off.

Lincoln felt unhurriedly in the pocket of his coat, bringing out Beasley's little .32 nickel-plated. He slipped it into the waistband of his pants.

'The girl,' he said to Coaley, 'is my property.'

Coaley's stare wavered and dropped. He whirled the watch leather.

'All right. Don't get excited.'

Lincoln turned to Ponch. 'Noticed you were a little slow getting off the train, Ponch. Shootin' out there didn't sound very appetizing, did it?'

It was a shot in the dark. But it hit. He knew that by Ponch's jaw working and the

74

unpleasant rumble of a laugh from Uncle Dock. Lincoln grinned tightly at the old man. He spoke as if the two of them had some understanding in common. 'It wasn't like that at Uvalde, was it, Uncle?'

'It sure wasn't, boy,' Dock muttered. 'It sure wasn't.'

Ponch cursed. 'It wasn't my fault.'

Lincoln walked close up to Ponch.

'The girl out there, Miss Ellis—You still made a water haul, friend.'

Ponch's eyes slitted. The fingers of his big right hand closed and unclosed. 'Who says so?'

'Link Jones.'

For a moment they traded appraisals of each other's size and strength.

Henny came to the door with the bottle and headed toward Uncle Dock.

Without looking away from Ponch, Lincoln reached, caught the bottle from Henny's hand, pulled the cork in one swift movement, and upended the bottle. He took a drag slowly, still looking at Ponch. It was rye and it burned and he liked the burn. He let his breath out to give Ponch some whisky secondhand. Ponch backed away one step.

Lincoln carried the bottle over to Uncle Dock.

'I can see what you mean, that you've been pretty hard up for men you can depend on.'

Uncle Dock took the bottle. He held his faraway look on Lincoln. 'You're one of my

75

best boys, Link. My best.' He stuck the bottle neck into his mouth.

Lincoln headed for the door, offering Coaley a flint chip of a smile, in case Coaley wanted to make friends with Uncle Dock's best boy. Coaley did. He flipped the thong, wet his lips, and said, 'I'll go out and help you fetch 'em in, cousin. Any friends of yours 're friends of Coaley Scull. You know how Uncle Dock is about kinfolks—thinks they ought to stick together!'

CHAPTER SIX

Coaley Scull dogged his tracks through the broomweeds. Clear, cold stars threw a faint light to the path leading from the house toward the corral. Lincoln went ahead of Coaley. He moved with a sense of unreality.

It was his impulse to overpower Coaley, to run, to make his escape in the night. But that would be senseless. They would ride him down in no time. And there were Beasley and the woman. He had brought them here. It was up to him to get them out.

He knew with hard certainty that the three of them had been roped and tied, from the moment he walked into the house. They were witnesses. Away from here, they would be the three who could describe, even call by name, the train bandits. Uncle Dock and these men would know that.

Coaley Scull said, 'I heard 'em talking, cousin. Where'd you leave them?'

'Corral. They wanted to stay out here till I went up to see who was at the house.'

Ten paces later, Coaley said heavily, 'Well, you saw.'

Lincoln slowed. Coaley slowed, too, and did not come up, but kept behind. Lincoln stopped and faced back to him.

'What about the old man? He's nearly blind, seems like. When did that happen?'

'He was that way when I joined up with them, down at Nuevo Laredo.'

'New with the bunch?'

'I been hanging around with 'em down there. That spread Uncle Dock's got in Mexico.'

'Took some planning, this one did.'

'Yeah. Uncle Dock sent me and Claude up ahead.'

'Uncle Dock—is he a little—sort of sick in the head?'

'Sometimes I think he is, then I think he's crazy like a fox. Like his eyesight. Don't let it fool you, he can see what he wants to see.' Then Coaley asked curiously, 'You used to ride with the bunch? When was that?'

'Quite a while back.'

'You-all pulled some big ones, I've heard. Uncle Dock likes to talk about 'em after he's likkered up. But I don't recollect hearing him

77

say your name.'

'He's a little absent-minded, Coaley. The way things stand, I better be getting along to where I was headed. Which was Fort Worth.'

'You got a deal there? I figured you was on the run. Ain't that what you said? You better stay with us, Link. We'll pull a new one mighty quick after this—Claude and Uncle Dock ain't going back to Mexico empty-handed.'

'Thing is, I got these two people out here. It'll be better for you-all if we keep moving. So suppose you just say *adios* to Uncle Dock for us and we'll borrow three of those horses in the pen and be getting along. You tell Uncle Dock that Link had important business somewhere else. Tell him it was better for me to take those other two people away from here.'

For a moment he thought Coaley was going to agree, but next he sensed the suspicion wafting off Coaley like a bad breath.

'You better talk to the old man about that.'

'That'd be all right, except Uncle Dock's a little hard to make understand a thing. You can see how it would be better for us to go on away from here.'

'We don't have three horses to spare,' Coaley objected. 'Nowhere you could go afoot, nothing but mesquite roughs in every direction.'

'We'll wait somewhere on the railroad. There'll be another train sometime.'

'You better stay here till Claude comes
78

back,' Coaley said shortly. 'Ponch and Henny wouldn't like it, anybody leaving here, knowing where this hide-out is and how we aimed to travel south. Uncle Dock would get mad at me and bust that whisky bottle over my head.'

Lincoln heard Coaley's voice trail off into a new and wary tone. Suddenly, the heavy-set form in the dark moved and a gun scraped the leather. The big Colt balanced in Coaley's hand.

'I catch on. You're worried about the filly, ain't you? That or something fishy. Well, you ain't going nowhere till we all leave. Don't try anything.'

With Coaley's gun pointed at him, a feeling came over Lincoln such as he had not known for many years. Hate not only for these men, but an old galling bitterness in his mouth for the trace of their blood in his own body. Something said, *Play it bad, like them, as befitting Dock Tobin's nephew, which is who you are, and which is the only language they understand.*

It was as if he shed one skin and put on another. He was all but engulfed with a lust to take Coaley's thick neck in his fingers and make the sound of life gurgle out of Coaley's thick-lipped mouth.

Dazedly, Lincoln worked his head and mumbled, shaken by his own thoughts. Coaley peered hard at him.

79

'How's that? You say something?'

'You got your gun in your hand.'

'You damn right.'

The reach of Lincoln's arm was deceptive, and longer by inches than Coaley could have expected. He twisted sideways, pulling Coaley forward, off balance. Strength and agility such as Coaley could never match whipped Coaley's right arm into the leverage of Lincoln's bent left elbow. Coaley cried out, stretching frantically to tiptoes and writhing against the last fraction of pressure that would snap the bone.

Lincoln held him so, for a long undecided moment. Then he dropped the wrist, placed an open palm in Coaley's heavy face, and shoved Coaley from him.

Coaley crouched and Lincoln picked up the six-gun from the path.

'What's my name?' he whispered.

'What?'

'Who you dealing with, *amigo*? Come on—if you got a brain, make it work. Say it—*say my name!*'

'It's—Link Jones.'

'Taste it good, Coaley.' He flung the words from his clinched teeth. 'Don't ever forget it. Say it again!'

'*Link Jones!*'

'All right.'

Lincoln moved in. He flipped the gun to change butt to muzzle and handed it to Coaley.

'Don't forget that name. It rode with the bunch at Uvalde and Sonora while you were still wet behind the ears. Don't pull a gun on me again, ever. Now you stick that gun in your diaper and stay here till I talk with those people down there.'

It was Dock Tobin's voice coming out of Lincoln's mouth, with a Dock Tobin ring of meaning in it, and Coaley halted.

'Well, but hurry it up. It's chilly out here.'

Lincoln reached the fence. Beasley came out of the shadows. 'What was that? We heard that talk! What did you run into here?'

Billie came and tried to see his face in the night.

He silenced Beasley. 'The train robbers are holed up here. Now don't start buckin', Beasley. You either, Billie. Just keep a hold on yourselves and listen to me. This is a roundup we can't just ride off from.'

Billie caught his arm. He felt her fingers tremble.

Beasley groaned. 'I told you we'd never make Fort Worth.'

Billie whispered, 'Is it bad, Lincoln?'

'Yes, it's bad.'

'It's—is it on account—because I'm here?'

She would be remembering, he knew. The way Ponch and Coaley had looked at her at the dry creek.

'Now you two listen. There's an old man here. The ringleader of this bunch. I used to know him. A long time ago. We're kin.'

'Kin!' Beasley echoed. 'Gaddly!'

'No use to fool you. This is a bad outfit. They planned that train holdup a long time, and it bogged down on 'em and they're mean. Now we got to go in that house.'

Billie asked fearfully, 'Can't we just *leave*?'

Beasley said hoarsely, 'Not Sam Beasley—I'm not going in that house. Give me my gun, Jones! I'm headin' for the mesquites!'

Lincoln fastened a fist in Beasley's coat.

'They'd run you down. We're afoot and we got nowhere to go. Don't act scared, but don't act smart aleck, either. You let me handle it and keep your wits about you.'

He felt the struggle die down in Beasley. The man edged closer to Lincoln, looking over his shoulder toward the house.

Coaley called from the dark, 'Hurry it up, Link! Let's go in and eat!'

Billie Ellis brushed at her clothes and lifted her chin to Lincoln. She made a small smile show up at him in the starlight.

'Lead the way,' she said. 'I'm used to rough audiences.'

'Not this rough, you're not. Now keep that beer-hall look off your face and your coat buttoned and let me do the talking!'

When they reached Coaley, Lincoln said, 'This is Coaley Scull. Kinfolks of mine. These two people had a little hard luck, Coaley. Like me. Got left by that hightailin' engineer.

Names are Billie Ellis and Sam Beasley.'

Coaley only grunted and fell in behind them.

'Pleased to meet you, Mr Scull,' Billie said coolly.

Beasley made sounds in his chest.

Lincoln led them in. The low adobe room was bathed in the yellow cast of a coal-oil lamp. Ponch Izaguirre squinted up from the bench. Dock Tobin stood before the fireplace. The hot smell of boiled frijoles and fried beef fogged in from the kitchen. The sound of the closing front door brought Henny to the curtain.

Dock Tobin lifted his massive head like an old buffalo scenting to windward.

'These two people are friends of mine, Uncle Dock,' Lincoln said. 'Miss Ellis and Mr Beasley. They'd like a little something to eat, and a place to bunk tonight. Then they got to head to Fort Worth.'

Ponch Izaguirre and Coaley stared at Billie. Dock Tobin fixed a long examination on them. He reached to the mantel, caught the whisky bottle, pulled the stopper. He ran the back of his hand across his mouth before the drink and after.

'Who told you to bring a woman to our hide-out, Link? You married to her?' Uncle Dock's voice was more curious than threatening.

'Couldn't help it, Uncle. They got left by the train, like I told you.'

'They'll be in the way,' Dock said thickly. 'In those wagons, when we head south. I don't like this.'

Henny spoke from the kitchen door. 'It's gettin' cold.'

Coaley had been watching Billie Ellis with unconcealed concentration. Lincoln observed the two spots of color showing in her cheeks. She kept her hands clasped composedly in front of her, and faced Uncle Dock.

'Say, I know you!' Coaley declared. His yellow eye flecks sharpened. 'The singer—I saw you, in a bar, somewhere.' He flipped the watch fob. 'The Longhorn Palace. In Crosscut. Didn't you sing at the Longhorn?'

'I've sung in a lot of places,' said Billie.

'The Girl with the Golden Voice,' Coaley quoted. 'Hey, Link, you really got yourself took up with a lot of woman there. How about a little song—'

'You gonna eat?' Henny demanded, 'or you want me to throw it out the winder?'

'You ought to hear her sing,' Coaley told Ponch.

'Yeah.' Ponch fingered his scar. 'Let's hear you sing us a little something.'

'I heard her,' Coaley said. 'I was in that Crosscut place, when Claude and me were there on this deal. She didn't look like she looks now. You'd of forgot every woman you ever knew, Ponch, even those chili-pepper brown ones down at Saltillo.'

84

Ponch pulled on his ragged mustache. He eyed Billie in hard raking examination.

Coaley was enjoying himself. 'She wore a fancy dress. Pink. You ought to have seen the way that crowd took on when she walked out to sing.' Coaley cut the yellow-speckled glance to Lincoln. 'Don't get sore, Link. I'm *bragging* on your gal.'

But Lincoln heard the mocking challenge. The treatment he had given the heavy youth outside would burn in Coaley's craw. He started to speak, to cut Coaley off, when Billie Ellis moved toward the bedroom doorway.

'Is there a mirror in there, Mr Scull? I know I look a fright, and I'd like to straighten myself up a little before we eat. Those awful mesquites out there—'

Ponch drowned out Coaley's first hasty words of protest.

'*Si! Si!* You go right in!' Ponch boomed. He closed one eye and grinned broadly. 'Go in there and get real pretty, Miss. There's a mirror, all right. Candle and matches on the table!'

She disappeared through the doorless opening, nodding a polite thanks to Ponch's invitation.

Henny muttered, 'You *bastard*, Ponch!'

Ponch waved a fat hand for silence, grinning. Coaley put a shoulder against the wall, watching the bedroom doorway. Lincoln felt Beasley edge closer to him. The fire log

85

made sputtering gasps and Uncle Dock turned to reach to the bottle on the mantel. 'She looks good,' Dock muttered. 'She'll ride in my wagon.'

A choked scream sounded in the other room.

Billie Ellis stumbled from the doorway, her hand clutching her throat.

Her eyes were wide and terrified, her face drained white. She rushed across to Lincoln with her pleading eyes raised to him. Then her head went down, almost touching his chest, and he felt wisps of her hair brush his chin. Her whole body was shaking.

'A dead man! Everything—*bloody!*'

Beasley's breath flew out in a rush. His mumble was drowned by the horse-neigh laugh from Ponch.

'Didn't take you long to pretty yourself in there!'

Coaley said tonelessly, 'Forgot to mention. That's Alcutt. This here's his nester place. We kinda moved in on him. Uncle Dock told him he could throw in with us and get rich, but he got sick on us and up and died.'

Uncle Dock angled a yellow-toothed grin around at them all.

Lincoln caught Billie by the shoulders, gently moved her from in front of him, and walked to the doorway. He stepped inside. The wavering candle flame on the table threw feeble light across to the cot in the corner. And he saw what Billie had seen. Alcutt. The bed and the wall and what was left of Alcutt's head.

Ponch came over, and Dock let him take the bottle.

'I told you to bury him, Link.'

Coaley laughed soundlessly.

Ponch came up from a long pull. 'He sure did, Link. Heard him myself.'

'That was Buckshot Withers, Uncle,' Lincoln said patiently. 'I already buried him.'

'You go dig a hole for him,' Dock said. 'Bury him out there where you buried Buckshot.'

They watched Lincoln. He said slowly, 'All right. I'll bury Alcutt.'

He turned to the others. 'One of you want to help me carry him out?'

Ponch, Coaley, and Henny stood silent and unmoving.

Lincoln's glance worked from one to the other, and finally to the wilting figure in the wrinkled green suit. Beasley stood with weight on his good leg, favoring the sprained ankle. His scared-rabbit eyes fled from Lincoln, then came creeping back.

'All right.' Beasley wet his lips. 'I'll help you bury him.'

'Let's eat,' Coaley said to Ponch.

Lincoln caught a protesting flutter of a white hand. Billie Ellis, her face pale, stood alone.

'You wanted a song.' Her voice was husky. 'All right—I'll sing. For—him, in there. Before you bury him, Lincoln.'

87

He saw her head lift, heard the small sound of her clearing throat. The first words came with difficulty, but then the trembling in them became controlled, and the words turned soft and clear. Soft, and sweetly vibrant, taking hold of the room, until only her voice existed in Lincoln's ear, and all else was dissolved, all the ugliness and all the hard staring faces. It made him feel that Alcutt was hearing it, too, these last sad words so gently sung here in the Ghost Ridge shack. Lincoln took his hat off, and stood with bowed head, because the beautiful words that came from Billie's throat were were known to him and he followed them faithfully in his mind as she sang.

'Lead kindly Light, amid th' encircling gloom,
　　Lead Thou me on!
The night is dark, and I am far from home;
Lead Thou me on!
Keep Thou my feet; I do not ask to see
The distant scene; one step enough for me...'

As her last words died away, her eyes came to meet Lincoln's, and held to him a moment. He saw the mist, and the fear. Silence hung over the room.

Dock Tobin raised the bottle.

'Mighty purty,' Henny said. 'Now come and get it.'

Lincoln murmured, 'Thank you, Billie—Sam, you ready?'

Dock Tobin lumbered around to Lincoln. 'Alongside where you buried Buckshot Withers.'

Coaley said complainingly, 'Hey, how about that funny one you sang, the one about the cowhand and the girl and the brown brindle bull? Remember that, all those funny verses?'

Uncle Dock said, 'Now get along with it, Link—I got a big deal to plan with you.' He raised his head and worked his sight to a tally of them all. 'With everybody—all my kin. We'll fix ourselves up for life, boys. That wasn't the only pile of money in Texas. The train got by us, boys, but the next deal will be a cinch. Then we'll all live it easy down south. Plenty of money the rest of our days. The whole Tobin bunch, with your Uncle Dock, and plenty of good Mexican *habanero* and whatever a man wants. We'll pull the damnedest big one Texas ever heard of, then we'll hit for that border and they ain't a lawman alive smart enough to catch us.'

He stalked to the kitchen doorway. Henny pulled aside. Uncle Dock went in. Ponch lumbered after him, then Henny.

Coaley said, 'Come get some plates of grub, Link. For you and your friends. Then you and the fat feller can lug Alcutt outside and directly I'll find you a spade. We'll bunk you three down at the barn—there's some blankets down

89

there. Better eat first, though—grave diggin' is damn hard work. Say, that song was right pretty, Miss Ellis—but I'd like to hear that sassy one, about the feller and the gal and the brindle bull.'

CHAPTER SEVEN

The Ghost Ridge site hadn't been picked for its natural beauty, for there was none, nor for any other reason that would ever make sense to anyone following after the first unknown nester. The yard was all thorn rootings and broomweeds, just as Lincoln remembered it. In the lantern light, the surrounding curtain of mesquites did not show, but they could be felt closing in the place.

Beasley, panting with the exertion of their load, exploded as soon as they were away from the house. 'Let's cut and run for it, Jones!'

'Don't be a fool, Beasley. You're not built for running.'

'I'm takin' out, damn you!'

'How? Afoot?'

'Any damn way I can get away from those fellers.'

'Go ahead, then. I'll dig two graves while I'm at it.' He knew that Beasley was going nowhere, alone.

Beasley's jumpy mind worked at that. He

was quiet for the rest of the distance of lugging their blanket-wrapped burden to the one sapling pin oak at the far edge of the clearing.

When Lincoln put the lantern down and took the first spade bite of earth, Beasley hovered close to him, away from the blanketed form.

'Don't it look softer over there on the other side of the tree?'

'Can't over there,' said Lincoln. 'That's Buckshot Withers.'

'Who's he?'

'Fellow that had the same trouble as this one.'

Beasley had been doing some thinking. He wanted to know, 'How come you're so savvy to all this outfit, Jones? Like those Tobins in there, and somebody being buried here? I never took you for a feller that'd been mixed up with them kind of people.'

The night air had turned cold. The packed *caliche* stubbornly contested Lincoln's muscles. He swung a pick and liked the jolt of it to his body and the way the exertions warmed him and loosened his joints.

One of the men came out of the shack with a rifle in his hand, unrecognizable in the weak lamp rays before the door closed. His shadow drifted off. A coyote yipped toward the ridge. From inside the house, the raised voice of Dock Tobin sounded momentarily, then all was silent again except for the rhythmic

91

thudding of the pick.

Beasley leaned against the tree. 'I was glad to get out of that house. Bringing him out here's upset my stomach. That supper didn't set well.'

Lincoln paid him small mind, being involved with the pick swinging, and with a digging of another kind. His brain chopped at a question like the pick point breaking the hard clods.

For a time, there in the house, and more especially when he had confronted Coaley, he had known a deep-stirring sensation that now was frightening as he tried to remember it. It had seemed that ten years of making the best dedication he knew how to shaping a respectable man out of himself, had somewhere left a gap. The gap had shown first when he had lied to the Crosscut marshal about who he was. It was the feeling of being *one of them*. This crazy day had plunged him back to something he could not fathom as he spaded out the clods in Alcutt's slowly shaping grave. It was like shedding a new and better skin, and putting on an old one that still fitted him easier, even though he hated the touch and filth of every scaly particle of its fabric.

Today, on his very first venture out of the new side of a life so painstakingly created for himself with Lucy's wise influence, the pendulum had swung all the way back across the years. A time or two, this day, and in the country he had once fled from, he had reverted to thinking like a Tobin. The cancerous truth spread all over him. He *was* a Tobin.

He was the same blood, bones, skin, and human that the people had once wanted dead bad enough to offer a thousand-dollar prize to the gun hand that would cause Lincoln Jones to decay in the clods like Buckshot Withers on the other side of the pin oak.

What did ten years mean?

What were the far-off Odessa spaces, or Lucy's deft guidance or the children's soft-eyed worship, or the time when he had been called on to lead the prayer meeting in the brush arbor at Clinkscale's place, vocally all thumbs at first, then secretly beginning to like it a little when he'd got the hang?

Out there in the lonely places, a man on a horse and with freshly finished creation about him had time to think. He could feel good thoughts inside himself, pick out his blessings to count among his hardships which were only the hungry-stomach and tired-muscles kind and had promise of betterment, and sometimes almost feel certain that he had been confidentially granted a secret glimpse of God's hand working in some quiet way. As when the prairie world hung still to let a sunset arrange and rearrange itself in a trying on of all the colors the Creator had to show. Or like the dark eyes of a beloved baby opening with awareness of life after the crisis of sickness. What became of all that, when a man found himself thinking to kill, like a Tobin outlaw again?

He had run off from the past, that time. That was all. The past still dangled here, as he was finding. Where it had left off. That old part of his life was a thing unfinished, like a short stretch of fence going a way and stopping, making no corners and no good ever to box anything in until finished foursquare and connected. His mind groped for a distinction, as he shoveled out the dirt. He had run away from the Tobins but he had never cleared it up with the world, nor himself, that he had been one of the clan by blood. He could get rid of that as he saw it, only by getting rid of the cause for it, which was the outlaws themselves. That was the only way to make the fence contain something, and he groped at this vaguely, sorting it out. Fate had given him the opportunity to avenge great evils, such as it had given not even to the lawmen who represented decent society and who had tried long and fruitlessly to track down the elusive Dock Tobin band. He'd better make up his mind—was he going to run away again and leave the snake crawling or stay and cut off its head? How was he going to do it? Without losing his own life, and maybe two others?

As an orphan waif thrown with the bunch, he had blindly, near crazily, wanted only to escape from the things he had known and seen. These were many. The way the bunch had needlessly shot the two scared bystanders in the Uvalde bank holdup. Uncle Dock, with his peculiar lust, and one of his swarthy lieutenants lashing him to a wall to make him watch their drunken raping of two sobbing Mexican girls in the house below the border. The desperate flight through the night with the posse on their trail after the trap that had been set for them in Del Rio. The hole-up days and nights when all the band had been drunk and fighting-mean, with curse words as thick as the whisky fumes. Knives striking at one another's stomachs in outbursts of accusations in the interminable poker playing with newly divided holdup loot. The casual way Uncle Dock had put his .45 to Buckshot Withers's head and triggered. And most of all, to the way Claude Tobin's flat eyes always looked when they rested on Lincoln as Claude would say to Uncle Dock, time and again, 'He's in the way, Uncle.' For a while, there wasn't a night but what he had lain in convulsions of fear that Claude was going to kill him before another morning came.

Those were things he had fled from. The questions stalked elusively about his mind— had he been delivered again into their hands? *Or had they been delivered into his?*

Beasley said, 'Ain't that about deep enough? You don't have to go to China.'

Lincoln stopped and mopped his face. He handed the spade to Beasley in the wavering lantern flame. 'You throw out a little of the

95

loose dirt. Spell me a minute.'

Beasley eased his flabby body into the hole and began pitching out the pick-loosened clods. A sorry helper he made, Lincoln thought, but felt no rancor against Beasley. Fine company to have, pitched into the middle of the Tobins like this. Beasley and the girl. Not that she wasn't all wool and a yard wide, more he'd seen of her. She had spirit and intelligence and strength, as well as a voice and looks.

Her being a woman made the problem what it was. If he had been saddled with Beasley only, he might head for the brush right now. He had the .32 revolver in his coat pocket and the night out there to hide in. He could take his chances at getting away and hiding until the bandits pulled out.

But not with the girl there in the house. Keeping her in there, as the gang would know, was the same as having the two men handcuffed to a tree. Either that, or they were mighty positive that there was nowhere to run off so that they couldn't be found in daylight. Even so, he had no doubt that one of them was out there somewhere in the dark, watching their work in the flickering lantern light, with a Winchester cocked for any funny move. Billie had to be gotten out of here, before he or Beasley could do a thing for themselves. He accepted that, and put his mind to a way to effect her escape, but nothing safe to try came to him.

Beasley gave up and crawled out, saying his hands were blistered. 'It's deep enough, anyway, Jones. Let's roll him in and get out of the cold.'

'Want to go back to the house? I can finish it.'

'No. Not till you go.' Beasley's teeth chattered. 'Damn it, Jones, how we gonna get out of this place? You reckon they'll let us go in the morning?'

'Help me lift him in.'

They lowered the blanket-tied remains of Alcutt into the shallow grave.

'You want to start shoveling the dirt in, Beasley?'

'I told you my hands got blisters big as quarters! This ain't my line. I don't want to throw no dirt down on a feller like that.'

'We all got it coming to us, some day.'

'Proper burial's one thing,' Beasley mumbled. 'Gettin' covered up like this without no coffin or anything, that's something else. Damn the Fort Worth & Chihuahua railroad to hell, anyhow!'

No, it wasn't proper burying a man with only a thin, bloody blanket over him and his boots sticking out. Even if he had tried to turn his hand at being a train bandit and had failed. Billie hadn't been ashamed to sing for the dead man. Lincoln tried to remember any words that might come to him, from the things that

97

Clinkscale had said at the occasional funerals at the brush arbor. They came in fragments, mixed up.

He took off his hat, concentrating. He looked hard at Beasley, against the tree, and Beasley straightened in a moment, and tugged off the faded fedora.

Lincoln murmured, 'Ashes to ashes and dust to dust. May God have mercy on your soul, Alcutt. Though we all walk through the valley of death, maybe you will find the—His rod and staff to help guide you, wherever you're going, in a way maybe you didn't think to use it here on earth. Now we lay you down to sleep. That's all I can think of to say over you, Alcutt. Amen.'

He put on his hat. 'Get to shovelin', Beasley.'

Henny materialized out of the night, with a rifle under his arm.

'Hurry it up and git that light out of the yard.'

'This kind of thing don't hurry much.'

'Let the little feller finish it. Ponch says Dock's waitin' on you in there. He's got some plannin' to do about tomorrow and he thinks you ought to be in on it.' Henny probed a little, showing his curiosity. 'Funny his favorite nephew ain't been around for so long. Reckon you been runnin' some big stuff on your own.'

'Don't let it worry you.' He stalked to the house.

Dock Tobin was planted bigger than

anything else in the room, watching Billie Ellis. He stood in the middle of the floor like a man in a trance, and did not turn when Lincoln came in.

Lincoln saw Billie sitting drawn up and white on the edge of a rawhide-bottom chair. Coaley leaned against a wall, his own eyes glazed a little, his big hand incessantly twirling the leather watch thong.

Billie turned a quick glance from Uncle Dock to Lincoln. He saw the appeal in it, and the thin trembling line of her tightened lips. She wasn't the kind to scare easy. She was scared now.

He stood inside the door, afraid that he knew.

Coaley quit flipping the watch leather. He gripped the butt of his leg gun. Lincoln realized that his first effort to make it stick that this was his woman had not registered very strong.

'Henny said you wanted to see me, Uncle Dock. About plans for tomorrow.'

Dock's mouth was sprung, a little moist and showing red in the gray field of whisker stubble. He held to a spread-out stance of waiting.

'You watch this now, Link. It'll make a man out of you. You and Coaley—Go on now, girl. Do it.'

Lincoln looked questioningly to Billie.

She said thinly, 'He wants me to undress.'

Coaley's eyes burned and he breathed

heavily like Uncle Dock. Lincoln checked this against the whisky bottle on the mantel. It had no more than a finger left. Coaley shifted, moving his hand into his side pocket and coming up with a knife. The spring button snapped loudly. The blade, sharpened to a white edge, flipped out. Coaley picked an edge of the door facing and sliced off a long finger of pine and began reslicing it into fine slivers, looking at Billie Ellis.

Dock laughed a noise like wet coughing. 'You goin' to pull 'em off yourself or you want me to have Coaley take 'em off of you?'

There was one other rawhide-bottom chair. Lincoln walked slowly between Dock and Billie, watching Coaley whittling at the sliver. He would have to turn his back on Coaley, when he sat, but that was a gesture of indifference he accepted. He would have to play this situation slow and lazy, like getting a rope on a wild horse. He stretched his long legs out loosely, at the same time bringing out tobacco.

'This is my girl, Uncle. I reckon you wouldn't want to josh her any more, this way. We better be planning our pull-out tomorrow. What time you expect Claude to get here?'

Dock shook his gray tousled head like dislodging a fly. 'You watch this, now, boy. You watch what we're goin' to take back home with us.'

He felt a small weight of Beasley's revolver

in his right coat pocket. The pocket of his Sunday coat was too small, his hand was too big, and the thing would be twisted and slow to get out. There was a better way, until he was ready, and he thought he knew how to handle it.

'Well, go on with the show!' he said harshly. 'Do what Uncle Dock told you, girl!'

The shocked look that Billie turned on him made his words gagging to his stomach. He held his stare hard on her while making a slow closing and opening of one eye. Billie's pale face had lost its rouge tints, and her hair ringlets had loosened, showing damp wispy ends. He saw her coat folded on the chair back. Her blouse had become disheveled, gaping a little at the buttons over the full swell of her fast breathing. Her expression changed from startled surprise to uncertainty. Her chin was still up in some inner hold on herself for spirit and dignity.

Lincoln fashioned his cigarette, watching her over his fingers as he sealed it. He made his movements easy. He held his gaze to Billie's as if he could poke the message across to her by force of vision. He had no thought but to take her side, to help her out of this. He was not her guardian, but the situation itself revolted him. He would stop it, simply because she was a woman in bad trouble and because he hated the pair in here who were taking it for granted that he was one of them, and would like this.

He tried to tell her that she ought to know he would have to side with these two, for the moment. Had to blunt the edge off the situation before he could do anything about it. The thing now, he wanted her to know, was to stretch it as thin as she could. He had to play against any crazy outbreak by the big man who watched her hungrily, or by Coaley trying to prove what a bad man he was.

'I can't do that!'

Billie shook her head slowly. Crimson spots came to her white cheeks. She looked like they had been badgering her a long time, he thought. She flung a quick look toward the door, then back to Dock. *Don't try that!* Lincoln had a frown ready for her. Coaley would run her down outside. Then it would be worse than in here.

Dock Tobin said in a coaxing rumble, 'Get up, now, pretty girl, and show us something.'

If she would only drag it out a little longer. If he could help her at all, he would have to do it as cautiously as riding around a Comanche camp.

But Billie flared up now, and he saw it coming. Anger and spirit flamed into her face and she crossed her arms in strained tightness across her bosom.

'Say something to the crazy old fool!' She flung the words at Lincoln. Her eyes brimmed. 'I can't stand this any longer!'

Coaley spoke behind Lincoln. 'Oh, yes,

you can.'

Looking at her now, caught in something she'd never dreamed could happen to her when she'd swished across the depot yard that morning, Lincoln remembered the way she and Beasley had gone into cahoots to try to fleece him. Well, the money was gone anyhow, and he was ruined, unless he recovered it.

'How'd a nice schoolteachin' job look to you right now, Miss Ellis?'

Her words rushed warmly across to him. 'Lincoln, I swear I'll never again stoop to do such a low thing as that the rest of my life, if you'll get me out of here. Please!'

'I'm glad to hear you say that. It was a bad thing, although the happenstance of the punishment seems a little severe.'

'You're all fools!' Billie wailed.

'They don't think so, necessarily. They been in the wilds a long time. Nobody's exactly a fool to want to see you—'

'Are you going to preach,' she demanded icily, 'or talk some sense into these drunken bums?'

Coaley said, 'Don't make so much palaver. You do what Uncle Dock told you!'

It was time now to try to haze the trouble to another pasture. The night was still ahead and he had to get himself out of here, and Billie with him. Coaley was dedicated to making himself hard to get along with. He wished heartily that he had knocked all the big white teeth out of

103

Coaley's oversized face when he'd been tempted to do so down at the corral. It was a chore to remember doing, next time the chance came handy and Coaley was feeling the big-man fever in his brain to play like Dock and shoot somebody.

Lincoln shifted his legs easily, took a long draw on the smoke, and dropped the butt to the floor. He pulled in his leg and ground out the sparks with a boot sole.

'All right,' he said. 'We'll put this off till some other time. How about a drink out of your bottle, Uncle? What's your plans on all of us pulling out of here tomorrow? Where we heading for? Who missed the big throw on that train job today? Coaley?'

He saw Dock's rigid stance relax and the slow turn of the heavy head toward him. For a moment, he thought he had succeeded. Dock was in the motion of turning back toward the rocking chair. Lincoln watched him, figuring that if Dock's mind had been diverted from this, it made no difference whether Coaley liked it or not. Dock lumbered around to the fireplace.

'We'll wait till Claude comes,' he muttered. 'We got to pull a big one before we go home. I'm glad you're back, Link. Maybe we're ready to try Byrd's Store. Claude will know.'

Lincoln heard Coaley's quick curse behind him. In the same moment, he knew with sickening clarity that he had misfigured

Coaley, for he heard his corduroys scraping like the slithering of a moccasin's belly across creek gravel.

When he tried to twist about and get out of the chair at the same time, it was too late. Coaley's heavy arm whipped around Lincoln's head, locking it against Coaley's shoulder. His rough palm closed over Lincoln's eyes. Coaley touched the sharp point of his knife against Lincoln's upstretched throat.

'Just move one inch!' Coaley gritted.

The blade pressured into his skin like a thing afire. Coaley's spread hand blinded him. Nothing existed but the bite of the pain at the tender spot, and the terrible knowledge of what one little jab by Coaley would do.

Coaley worked his fist. The knife point hurt. The pressure was too hard. His nerves screamed for him to try to strike the knife away and his reason had to fight against the insanity of moving.

'Take the knife away, Coaley.'

Coaley said, 'He tried to outtalk you, Uncle Dock. He thinks he's a slick 'un!'

Coaley showed Billie his fist making a small circle with the knife handle. 'What'd you rather do, girl, take your clothes off or see me stick him?'

The effort to stay perfectly still was almost too much. He wanted to struggle. He concentrated so hard to keep from trying to break away from the small burning spot of

105

pain that his body hurt all over. He tried, very slowly, to move his neck away from the knife, but the knife hand caught on to this. Coaley made the pressure follow, and the knife hurt as much as ever. Now there was no farther slack to give in his twisted neck muscles.

Coaley spoke gloatingly across to Billie. 'You want to see me do it?'

Lincoln heard the sounds of Billie getting up from the chair. Terror was in her whisper. 'No! Don't, Coaley!'

He mimicked, *'Don't, Coaley!* Hey, Jones, how's this feel?' The point bit deeper.

Billie's voice caught with a sob. 'Mr Tobin, *please*, can't you do something?'

Dock chuckled. 'They're just horseplayin', girl, never saw two cousins that didn't want to scuffle each other like studs in a pasture. You ought to see our crowd when it's all together. That Coaley's a smart one.'

The knife point eased, then came back. Lincoln gritted, 'Not so hard, Coaley.'

He couldn't stand the knife point much longer. It was all that he could do to resist the crazed necessity to try to throw himself out of the chair.

Coaley spoke in his ear. 'How you liking this, big cousin? Ain't so much stuff on the end of a stick now, are you?' Coaley was proud of this. This was showing something, to himself and to Uncle Dock and to the girl. Coaley Scull was somebody to have along.

106

He played the knife handle back and forth as if working the point in. Lincoln could hear his own gagging breath like a man going down under chloroform.

Through the shrill ringing pain he heard the soft rustling of Billie's clothing. Her words came resigned and low. 'All right, Coaley.'

Coaley laughed, pleased with this great thing he had achieved for Uncle Dock's pleasure, and making sure that Dock knew where the credit belonged.

'Watch this now, Uncle. She's gonna undress.'

Lincoln felt the point of the knife ease a trifle, but the sharp bite was still there. Coaley's left arm still encased his head in a powerful twist, making the strain on his stretched neck and throat hurt so much that his tight clinched eyelids began to flash red-hot sheets.

Dock said irritably, 'Be careful with that knife, Coaley. She's Link's woman. When she undresses you treat her nice. Just look, that's all.'

Coaley's voice spoke a hoarse order to Billie. 'Undress *slow.*'

One shoe dropped to the plank floor, then the other, and he heard her stockinged feet on the boards. There was no sound at all for a moment, but his own choking breath. The burning sheets of pain poured over him in waves of molten hate for his grotesque state of helplessness, for the shame that had befallen

107

Billie, and the one sure separate hate for Coaley Scull that strengthened him for enduring this so that he could live to kill Coaley.

The gunshot, outside the window, and the double crashing of glass there and at the fireplace, were like explosions in the stupor of his tortured brain. But Billie's short scream was not imagination, nor the way Coaley jumped back, releasing the knife pressure and his hold on Lincoln's head. Lincoln plunged sidewise from the chair, rolling across the floor and catlike to his feet with his hand fighting to drag out the revolver. Coaley crouched, facing the shattered window glass with his six-gun raised. Uncle Dock held his gun in his hand, too. Billie Ellis, in stocking feet and blouse unbuttoned, was grasping it closed over the fullness of her camisole as she stared wide-eyed, first at the broken window, and then at the whisky-bottle pieces where they had smashed on the hearth.

'We're raided!' Dock broke into long strides to the door and into the night. Coaley rushed after him. Outside Dock bellowed, 'Ponch! Henny!'

Lincoln nodded to Billie because his throat felt paralyzed, meaning to indicate that she was to fix her blouse and put on her shoes. But before she did either, she ran across the bare boards to him and threw herself hard against him, with her hands clutching at his arms and her lips trembling in her drained face. She burrowed her head into his chest and he could feel the tremors all over her body. Her smothered words sounded where warm tears moistened through his shirt. 'I'm scared, Lincoln! *Scared!*'

CHAPTER EIGHT

The life of a singer in the Texas frontier towns had been no bed of roses for Billie Ellis. Still, as she sometimes said for self-reassurance, it paid for a single bed, which was better and which was more than some girls could say for the jobs *they* had. And there were elements of pleasure to it if one was so constituted as to overlook the hardships. A woman could not be unaffected by the way every man's eyes rushed to her like steel dust to a magnet, holding to her looks, and to her singing, with the whole smoky room turning quiet and whisky glasses forgotten. She was no Lily Langtry, she knew, but her looks seemed to suffice for the job and her voice was serviceable if she took pains with the high notes.

She could make them look sad and remembering, their sight going misty, with her tremulous singing about lost love or mother or the wrong hanging of a good boy in a lonesome country. And she could change all that to grins on their hard, wind-dried faces and put jig urges in their feet, with the bold numbers. It was fun to make them yell, finally, for the one they liked best, about the cowhand and the girl and the brown brindle bull.

On Saturday pay night, there would be the fold of currency from the owner in his back office, to be poked down into the natural pocket inside her camisole, and the routine resistance against the owner's hand wanting to follow his money. This could be done with reasonable poise, unless he was staggering drunk. Then a girl could choose her weapons as needed.

The ones she had to watch were the dignified bankers and store owners, or the big, genial cowmen who exuded the chivalrous protector through every pore like their perspiring rye. All they wanted for their knighthood in championing a pretty saloon singer was to come over to your room after the place closed, for just a nightcap together and a little talk, which soon took the direction that with them it would be all right because they were gentlemen.

She had learned to be wary of any man who habitually wore a coat and big watch chain and to do without their championing, in favor of managing things her own way. The piano players, a breed alone, were always the same, and as predictable to her as their left-hand chords. They were drunk by midnight, and had the same mournful-eyed assumption that because you worked together and were both musicians there oughtn't to be any little petty differences between you, such as a hotel-room wall.

In these five years of trouping out of her twenty-five, she had found one town much like another. Exciting to arrive in and get started, and just as exciting when leaving on the journey to the next.

She had begun to wonder a little, secretly, when the years were going to produce the one man she would want as a husband out of all the thousands of men in the towns. A girl began to feel a hidden concern as time rolled along, for the dim corridors of life ahead were not too inviting, faced alone, and she felt sure there was abundant love in her heart and body waiting to be poured out forever to the man she would marry, if ever the right one would come into her life and make himself known. So far, this illusory mate was still without form or features, and she only knew he was not one of the innumerable suitors who had proclaimed their love and stated their offers. These she had sympathetically had to reject, for one fancied defect or another, with nothing materializing from any courtship but her fading recollection of it, like old signposts in her memory to mark the towns.

And so, after each stay had run its course, there came the day of knowing that it was time to move. You had used up your appeal in a place, or the owner had booked a new girl, or a drought was on and business was rotten, or you had played out your percentages of being able to cope with the boss, or the pianist, or you were simply fed up with a town and ready for the next one.

Not that it would be any different. The same up-turned faces again, same thoughts behind them, same smoke fog over the hall and bar smells and the sooty lamp chimneys. Another owner with hands, and a sad-eyed keyboard professor with the same bass chords and an instinct for exactly the right moment to wander into your dressing-room when you were changing.

The Longhorn had been no different, and once the decision to move was made, she had found the leaving almost as exciting as arriving, for she had decided, on whim, to head east for Fort Worth and a short vacation.

Yesterday, there had been packing to do, errands of various kinds that went with leaving a place and starting a long trip, good-bys to be said to a few friends at the Longhorn and over the town. Buying the new satin suit at the City Mercantile had been an expensive indulgence but an enjoyable one, and finding the exactly right hat to go with it a small miracle. The stage dresses took careful folding and packing in the trunk before its loading on Blackmon's dray for the haul to the depot.

Then morning, with train day actually dawning. Travel shoes clicking their last good-bys along Crosscut's plank walks, spring shining green and clean out in the prairies, and many day-coach hours ahead in which to just sit and see the empty country without a single yellow-toothed smirk or red eye or brandished six-gun anywhere in the audience.

No sadness in leaving. No regrets at all in her last glance back at the tall frame front of the Longhorn, where the new-painted sign already blurred out her name and *The Girl with the Golden Voice*, in favor of one Hazel Daley, *Songs Like You Like 'Em*. No regrets, only a jauntiness and gaiety under the dressy lines of her new suit and its frosting of the little veiled hat, but with such feelings properly restrained in secret places beneath a lady's dignity.

She had wanted to laugh when, tripping around the depot corner, she had almost walked into the angular man with the valise who was stopped to look at the engine. That had struck her as funny and she might have laughed with him at their near collision if he had shown any sign of joining in. One sidelong glance at such a serious face and the dark Indian look of his eyes had stayed the laughter, and she had gone on her way taking pains to make it appear she had never noticed him. For one who looked on men by the dozens every night, in a mass of smoke-blurred faces like sheep in a pen, it was hard for her to say why

113

she made a conscious effort to see this tall leather-faced stranger again.

But she knew when he conversed with Sam Beasley. She saw him in brief conversation with Marshal Kincaid, sensing from nothing more tangible than intuition that he was uncomfortable in whatever was being said. And she knew with certainty, and was not displeased, that he studied her from his seat in the day coach.

Just why she had ever agreed to Sam Beasley's proposition that she pretend to be a schoolteacher, she would never know. Sam was such a crooked little card sharp, ousted from one place and then another, and finally clear out of town by Marshal Kincaid's stern edict. But he was a hard one to outtalk, once he got his slick words going, and there was a promise of good money in it, Sam had said, and a little innocent fun. It was never clear in her own mind whether her moment of weakness had been the result of the money prospect, or the circumstance offered to make the acquaintance of the man Sam called 'Odessa.' She would let herself go a little way into it, she had boldly decided, at least until she knew the stranger and understood what Sam was getting at. If Beasley's obscure scheme turned too rough for her liking, she could always wash her hands of both Sam and the scheme.

During the half hour or so that the train

would be stopped for fuel wood, she could just as easily have stayed in her seat. But the mesquites looked pretty and green, there was exercise to be had, walking down to the dry creek while the men loaded wood, and perhaps the chance that she would appear to accidentally wander upon this man, Lincoln Jones, and walk back with him and his wood load. But Jones headed off with strides nobody but a horse could match, going far out to the last scattering of cut wood. Beasley trailed off, too, and both lost themselves down the brushy gully. And in the next little while was when her pleasant day began to go to pieces and smash in fragments around her like the explosion of a bullet-blasted hanging lamp.

The shooting, the horrible bandits, all the commotion and the minutes of her terrified hiding—those were unbelievable nightmares, capped off by the dismal realization that the train had left her. She had been confronted with bad moments before now, but this was a predicament that was maddening and a little frightening. At first she felt stunned disbelief that such a thing could happen to her. Then, with bleak acceptance of the awful fact that she was stranded, her trouper's instinct took hold for making the best of it. She concealed her misery and misgivings behind an outward calm and told herself that the resourceful-looking Odessa man would somehow get them out of this.

His own worry, according to the hard set of his lean jawlines, must have been greater than her own. Yet he bore a sort of granite steadiness about him that spread a little to her and Beasley, and before she knew it she was concerned with whether she could measure up to the qualities this man would expect others to show in a troublesome circumstance.

The rest of the day was bad enough, walking through the rough country, though she had found herself drawn to unfathomable liking for the quiet-spoken man. Tonight, coming into the house with the outlaws, was worse than all the rest combined. Everything was confused and threaded with the terrible undercurrent of distrust and danger. It was confusing to try to understand exactly just who Lincoln Jones was, what his connection might be to these men, and she knew that Beasley was as mystified as she was.

But now, in the last half hour, all thoughts had fled from her mind but the terrible dawning of what the old man and the young man meant to make her do. She had tried flippancy, cajolery, haughtiness, and meanness, without denting their crudely spoken intentions. She was determined to control her mounting hysteria, and when she thought that Coaley was going to cut Lincoln's throat before her eyes, she no longer had strength for resistance. She resigned herself dully to doing whatever she had to do. For if they killed Lincoln Jones, they would kill Beasley, too, and she would be alone with the Tobin outlaws.

With no feeling except the pounding blood of shame burning her face and fear icy in her fingers, she slipped off her shoes. As she began to unbutton her blouse, her brain caught at one small glimmer of a way that might help Lincoln to get free. She would take off the blouse, and she would make herself smile archly at Coaley, and move slowly toward him as she stepped out of her skirt. And she would be within reach of him when she began to loosen her camisole. Then, or when she began to expose herself down to bare flesh, Coaley likely would never be able to restrain his hands from reaching for her. If he would only take the knife away, for just an instant, Lincoln could wrench himself away, she hoped. She had almost come to the moment to force herself to smile invitingly at Coaley, when the bullet cracked through the window and she thankfully saw Lincoln dive to the floor out of Coaley's grasp.

*   *   *

Sam Beasley's life had been devoted, as far as possible, to avoiding situations that might call for a man to show strength of morals or muscles, for Beasley had little of either and knew it. The big money, the big games, the big deals and the ability to face the dangerous

117

showdown moments with hardcase customers were for stouter operators than himself and they were welcome to it. There was a living of a sort to be had on the crumbier outer fringes, and if it was a shabbier existence, by comparison, it was all he felt equal to and he had no illusions about his limitations for doing better. The small game, small cheating and the unelaborate confidence scheme were appropriate to a shyster of his stature, and if the gains were never very large, neither were the dangers.

When a few small-time victims had mouthed their complaints to Marshal Kincaid, the Crosscut lawman had not even done him the dignity to take his feet off his desk when he sent for Beasley and told him to leave town. Kincaid had done this with the insulting manner of small annoyance that he might have shown in sliding a dozing hound out of his doorway with the scrape of his boot. Beasley had no argument to make with the marshal, he had known such farewells before, and he had been prompt about telling the loafers around the Longhorn that he had been called to Fort Worth on important business. After that, it was only a matter of keeping out of Kincaid's frowning sight until train day, and then bidding adieu to another town that had decided it didn't want him among its citizenry.

Running into Lincoln Jones had appeared to be a stroke of luck. He quickly scented easy pickings if he could think of a slick way to handle it. His impromptu scheme was enhanced by the chance presence of Billie Ellis, and Beasley began to speculate that his exit from Crosscut might have its silver lining after all. His first snap impression that Jones would be an easy one soon changed into a more cautious knowledge that this would be a bad customer to handle if he got riled, but that was where Billie's role would come in.

Whatever the prospects might have been, they went to pieces in Beasley's mind when the terrible thing happened at the wood stop. His day was ruined, the silver lining with it.

His state of mind had grown steadily worse during the tortuous walk through the eternity of mesquites. No matter what Lincoln Jones said, nor Billie's forced optimism, something told his worrying mind that this was one he would never get out of. In the house tonight, in the actual presence of the murderous bandits, this fear gnawed right into his marrow and all but paralyzed him. He tried to make himself as small and drawn as possible when one of the bad men looked his way and he stuck close to Lincoln. All at once the Odessa man seemed like his best friend in the world.

With the creepy burying finished, Beasley watched uneasily as Lincoln walked toward the shack. He would have followed at his heels, except that remaining outside with Henny seemed better than being inside with Dock,

Tobin. He tried to make conversation with Henny, but his words trickled out disjointedly. Henny ignored the offer. Beasley morosely ambled without direction. Henny extinguished the lantern. Every time Beasley glanced over his shoulder in the ghostly starlight, Henny was a sauntering shadow behind him with the rifle under his arm.

Beasley did not know whether he wandered up to the window light by accident or for the purpose of looking in. The night air had him shivering. He wished Jones would come back outside. It was creepy out here, but creepier around that Dock Tobin. What he saw when he first glanced through the window glass was a tableau of such unreality that he could only stare, stunned and disbelieving. Billie stood in the middle of the floor in her stocking feet, unbuttoning her blouse. Dock Tobin, a gaunt gray animal who frightened Beasley limp just to see him, stood near the fireplace. Through the dirty windowpanes Coaley appeared to be working a knife blade into Lincoln's throat and Beasley held his breath waiting to see the blood gush out.

Henny spoke behind him. 'I'll be damned!'

Beasley made a dying-frog croak.

Henny said, 'Watch this now. Dock's gonna make her undress.'

Beasley shuddered.

'Ponch's luck to be out at the corral. He'll be mad as hell, missin' this.'

120

Beasley had eyes only for Coaley's knife. He was only vaguely aware that Henny had come up close behind him. Both of them stood stooped a little to see through the small window.

All his life, Beasley had shied from the big moments of crisis, the necessity to do something conclusive or dangerous or physically hard to do. He knew no lust to kill Coaley nor any call to make some heroic move to protect Billie. The desperation that flogged him like a quirt was the blind need to look out for himself. He would be lost if they killed Lincoln. He'd be alone with the outlaws, in a hell of a shape. He was like a drowning man and Jones in there was a raft to grab at and was about to slip out of reach. Beasley's brain caught fire. He whirled on Henny, grabbed the rifle from Henny's arm, shoved Henny back with a desperate thrust, and turned the rifle toward the window, all in one exploding movement. He could not aim at Coaley for fear of shooting Lincoln, and he had to make the bullet miss Billie. The only target, then, was Dock Tobin. He had to shoot at *something*. He simply put the rifle to his shoulder, pointed the waving end toward Dock, and pulled the trigger.

Lincoln shot across the floor, and Beasley had the awful belief that the bullet had hit Lincoln. But the Odessa man bounded erect and pulled a revolver out of his pocket, and

121

Beasley felt relieved. Like a man casually returning a borrowed tobacco pouch to a stranger, he thrust the rifle back to Henny, feeling his knees turning to water, and stood shaking. Coaley and Dock plunged around the corner. Beasley's body sagged, waiting for the storm to break upon it for this thing he had done. Dock and Coaley flourished their guns and Dock growled, 'What the hell was that, Henny?'

Ponch showed up. 'What's the shootin'?'

Coaley shoved Beasley out of his way and looked at the splintered glass.

Henny pointed. 'He done it!'

For an awful moment Beasley felt the four sets of outlaw eyes on him. Henny made a nervous chuckling. 'I gave him the gun, Dock, to hold while I made a smoke. That's all it was. The damn thing went off just as I handed it to him.'

With agility that stupefied Beasley, Dock swung his mammoth shoulder and arm and knocked Henny down.

'You ruined a damn good show and broke my whisky bottle.'

Coaley tugged at the old man. 'We can start it over, Uncle.'

'He ruined my notion, too.'

'What was going on?' Ponch demanded.

Coaley mocked, 'Wouldn't you like to know?'

'Wouldn't you like to get out here in the cold

and stand lookout for a while?'

Henny, still on the ground, looked up at Dock. 'It was just an accident. Don't get sore about it, Dock.'

Dock spoke mournfully, his head lifted to the night. 'Not enough sense in the whole bunch to pull that holdup. Not enough sense to keep from shooting out the window. I'll show you something—I'm putting Link and Claude in charge from now on. They'll make you have a little sense.' Dock looked at them with eyes that could see well in the dark and hefted his six-gun. Nobody moved.

'Henny, get some bedrolls out of the wagon for these new people and bed 'em down in the barn. You and Coaley and Ponch take turns on lookout tonight. I'm goin' to bed.'

Coaley and Ponch moved off with nothing to say. After Dock rounded the corner Henny got up.

'Listen, feller, that gun just went off! You hear that?'

Beasley's teeth chattered. 'All right, all right.'

'If Dock knowed I let you grab it out of my hand, he'd have been mad at me.' Henny cackled unpleasantly. 'Don't you never tell it different, or I'll cut your ears off!'

That suited Beasley fine. 'By gaddly, I'm a man you can trust, Henny!' He heard Lincoln's voice and hurried around the house to find him.

123

Lincoln stood just outside the door with the lamplight weakly etching his long jaws harder and his eyes blacker than Beasley had ever seen them. It showed the nickelplated revolver still in Lincoln's hand. He heard Dock saying, 'You wasn't much use to us before, boy. You look like you could do something now, and I've got plenty for you and Claude to do. I ain't got the outfit I used to have, Link.' The big head rose. His filmy eyes searched the night. Dock was seeing something far away. Billie pressed close to Lincoln. Coaley emerged from the darkness and stopped. Dock muttered, 'We ain't going back empty-handed. We'll hit Byrd's Store and if we're lucky that'll be a big one.' He shuffled inside, and Lincoln looked to Coaley, and quickly across to Beasley and down at Billie's face, as if tallying up the worst of several problems.

'No hard feelings, Link?' Coaley followed Dock, walking half sideways. 'That was just a little rawhidin', cousin. I wasn't gonna stick you.'

Lincoln turned toward the corral without replying to Coaley, except for a look that followed Coaley into the house. Billie walked beside him and Beasley hurried, keeping close to Lincoln. He told them how it had happened, a picture that grew in Beasley's mind with the telling. By gaddly, he had overpowered Henny against great odds. His knees still felt like water, but he had become an important man,

124

and Lincoln and Billie were thanking him for what he had done. 'I would have wiped out the whole clan singlehanded,' Beasley heard his own tongue assuring them, 'but I was having to fight Henny off all the time I was aimin'.' He had done a big thing. Biggest thing in his whole life, he guessed. He wished a bunch of Crosscut birds could have seen the way he bucked all these outlaws.

The corral, two wagons, and the shed showed up gloomy as death. Beasley's moment dimmed out like a spent candle. He walked closer to Lincoln and wished that he had stayed to be locked up in Kincaid's Crosscut jail.

CHAPTER NINE

The low-raftered shed room hung heavy with the smell of old harness and stale hay. Henny came to the door with three bedrolls from the wagon and a lighted lantern.

Lincoln asked, 'What time you cooking breakfast?'

''Bout daylight, I reckon.'

'Don't forget you got two extra people to feed. That'll be Beasley and me. The lady won't eat till later.'

'There'll be plenty of grub. We come well stocked.'

Henny backed out the door, reeling in his

eye line from the girl, who relaxed to a bedroll and leaned against one of Alcutt's bales of hay. Lincoln moved the lantern until he sighted what he had hoped to find in the shed—a saddle and bridle hanging on a wall peg. After making a measuring appraisal of Billie's outstretched legs he unbuckled the stirrup leathers, shortening the straps up to the last notches on each side. In a corner he found a ragged saddle blanket and put it with the worn saddle. It would be dark in the pen and he would have to take the horse he could catch the easiest, trusting that it was not too wild and wouldn't buck with a woman.

He ached with a monumental tiredness in all his bones. His neck still hurt from Coaley's twisting hold on it and there was a dull burning where the bullet had grazed his arm. He spread a bedroll for Billie in the far corner on the other side of the hay bales. When he stooped to arrange his own across the room, Beasley, who had silently watched his movements, made a thumb motion toward the saddle.

'What's that for?'

Lincoln tilted his head toward Billie. 'Her.'

Billie sat up. 'For riding or for a pillow?'

Beasley shot to his feet. 'Just her? Why can't we all go?'

'Because we'll be eating breakfast up at the house with them. It's our best chance to get her out of here.'

'By gaddly, I'm riding, too.'

126

'With you and me here, we've got a chance to cover for her while she gets away. If either one of us was out of pocket, they'd have somebody with a Winchester out looking.' To Billie he said sharply, 'Are you up to it?'

'I guess so,' she said with great weariness. 'Anything will be better than here.'

He murmured, 'You did all right up there. You, too, Beasley.'

She lowered her blue gaze from him and rested her chin in her hands. 'I'll see that knife in my sleep the rest of my life.'

'It was a bad thing for you.' He touched a finger to the smarting spot in the skin of his throat. She had been brave and steady, all right.

Billie asked, 'Where will I ride to?'

'We'll saddle a horse before daylight. Beasley and I will go up to breakfast. If I don't come right back out the door, you'll know they're all inside. You go through that little feed door to the stall, get on the horse, and ride out north. Keep the shed between you and the house. When you get in the mesquites, circle back south, the way we came up here today. You think you can do that?'

She nodded, listening closely.

'You'll hit the railroad directly. From then on, follow the tracks west. I don't know how far you'll have to go until you find somebody. Maybe all the way to Crosscut. I figure it's closer back to Crosscut than it is the other way

127

toward Eskota.'

'If I—When I get to Crosscut, what should I do then?'

'Go to the law. Tell them what this is back here. Tell them the Tobin bunch tried the holdup, and that they're traveling south in two wagons. Tell them that they plan to hit Byrd's Store—that's a stage station four or five days south of here by wagon. If they get a move on and get a posse headed this way, they can catch the outfit before that, though.'

'I'll be afraid.' She smiled weakly. 'But there's nothing else to do, is there?'

Beasley asked him, 'What will you and me do, Jones? After she leaves?'

The same question plagued Lincoln, but he could not let Beasley see that. How could he explain when he was racked himself by conflicting emotions whirling him around like a windmill wheel?

Beasley hurried to scent trouble. 'Now, look here, Jones, you're not figurin' on violence with them? You wouldn't stay around this graveyard just to try to get even with Coaley, would you?'

'Nobody could get even with Coaley without killing him,' Billie commented.

Yes, he wanted to kill Coaley, that he knew. But there was more to it. He said slowly, 'I'm not a killing man, not one to kill in cold blood, at least. Even Coaley.'

'Thought all you Odessa people were
128

bloodthirsty, way I always heard it.' Beasley grimaced. 'You know what they call you, back here?'

Billie said, studying Lincoln, 'Maybe the breed has played out, Sam. Maybe there just aren't any more of those invincible Texas gunmen any more.'

'We have a few show up,' Lincoln said. 'There's one comes hellin' it up once in a while waving his reputation for being one of those invincible quick-draw killers, like you mention.'

'What became of them?'

He smiled briefly at her. 'They got killed.'

'Not so invincible, after all, then?'

'Most any bullet will shoot through a reputation. Any man can get himself killed, if he goes around asking for it.'

'Well, did Coaley ask for it?'

'Coaley asked for it twice. With you and with me.'

Billie's eyes softened. 'I'll live over that little stunt back there. I just want you and Sam to keep from getting hurt. I hope you'll clear out of here just as soon as I'm gone.'

'That's what I say!' Beasley nodded. 'Already seems like I been here a year.'

There was something besides killing Coaley, and better. But he did not know how to express it, because his own feelings struggled at cross-purposes within himself. What he wanted, he thought, was to turn the Tobin bunch in to the

129

law. That was something that might balance off the bad years. And just as much, he wanted to get away. The urgency prodded him to get on the trail of his Odessa money. Without the money recovered the outlaw taint would follow him and hurtful talk would break out. People would begin to whisper that Jones had stolen their money, and it would near kill Lucy because she, too, would always wonder in her secret mind.

'We'll get away, I guess,' he said, finally answering Beasley. 'After Billie's gone.'

'Dock seems to think you're back to join up with them,' Billie remarked.

'He can be fond of a man one minute and shoot him through the head the next. He's a little confused about me.' He wondered how Dock would take it when he found that he had sent Billie away.

As if he, too, had been thinking of Lincoln's strange role with the bad men, Beasley suddenly asked, 'What kind of a feller is this Claude they're looking for?'

No use making Beasley any jumpier than he already was, but no use to fool him, either.

'He's bad.'

'Worse'n these?'

'I'd say about double.'

'I don't like that. Not a bit.'

Lincoln spoke to Billie. 'You better be getting what sleep you can.'

'Who could sleep?' She shivered. Fingers of

chill wind reached through the cracks in the walls and played with the dust and straw.

Beasley mumbled, 'Like as not get our throats cut, all of us.'

Lincoln took the lantern to the feed door in the side wall. 'Let's take a look out here, Beasley. We want to know what we're doing in the morning when we try to get a mount saddled for Billie. It'll be dark then.' He unsnapped the spring latch and lowered the door. Holding the lantern aloft, he looked through into the rail horse stall built against the shed.

What he saw, piled in a jumble in the feed trough just below the opening, caused him to whistle softly, then call back to Beasley.

'Come here and hold the lantern! Here's our baggage off the train!'

'What?' Beasley limped over with one shoe off.

Lincoln handed the lantern to Beasley and reached through. He began lifting assorted valises and telescope bags inside to the floor. Hopefully, he took a quick look at each one as he pulled it inside to the light.

He heard Billie call eagerly, 'That one's mine! How on earth did they get here?'

Lincoln was hoisting the last one through, having to reach far down to the bottom of the hay rack to find it. Recognition flooded warmly over him as he lifted the valise inside.

He grinned broadly. 'There it is! That's

131

mine!'

His hands shook a little as he dug into it. The holstered gun and belt were there. He pawed under his spare clothes, felt the bottom of the bag, and when his groping fingers did not touch the money belt he took out all the contents, one piece at a time, until he knew the truth.

He repacked his things, all but the gun. He pulled the old Colt out of its holster and looked to the cartridge loads in its black chambers. He buckled on the gun belt, keeping his back to the others, not wanting his disappointment to show.

The gun was something to get back, at least. But the money loss—that was a blow. The full meaning drained him hollow. The fact stood out to cut him adrift, a man without destination, with no purpose now in trying to get to Fort Worth and unable to see himself returning home and trying to live down the loss.

Billie called quietly, 'Did they take your money, Lincoln? It's gone, isn't it?'

'Seems to be missing.'

'How much was it?' Beasley wanted to know.

Lincoln said, 'More than you could ever count, Beasley. This money wasn't just in dollars.'

'What did they do?' Billie asked. 'How did the bags get here?'

132

Lincoln sat and rolled a cigarette. 'Ponch threw the bags on the far side while everybody was out of the coach. That's what they came back for, after the train left. They probably had a pack horse, then when they got here they just unloaded 'em in the stall when they unsaddled.'

'But wouldn't they divide your money and whatever else they found?'

'I aim to find out.'

Beasley bristled. 'Now, we ain't stayin' around here while you wait to find your money. Nosiree, Jones!'

'Your situation's a little different from his, Sam.'

'The hell it is. I buried one dead man tonight, and all I got to say the next one ain't gonna be Sam Beasley.'

Lincoln gazed down hard at Beasley, and the little man's jumpy eyes scurried. 'All right, Beasley. We'll not invite trouble on that account. There's nothing to be done about it, anyhow.'

'Then we gonna get out of here, soon as Billie's safe away?'

'Yeah. We'll get out.' They might as well run for it, as soon as the chance offered. The job was too big for him. Just going to Fort Worth with the Odessa money had been too big for him, also. He had made a complete fizzle out of everything. Like in the house, with Coaley torturing him and making him helpless while

133

they tried their special brand of taking wicked, lustful advantage of a woman. Worse than a band of drunk Comanche bucks with a female captive. They were the strong Tobins. He was the weak one. Now, as when he was a kid.

Billie said suddenly, 'I'll never be able to ride a saddle in this skirt! Sam, you're the smallest—have you got an extra pair of pants in your bag? If you have, get them out. A shirt and coat, too!'

Beasley grudgingly handed the clothes over to her. Billie said, 'You two turn your heads.' She went around the hay bales to the shadowed corner. For the second time that night, Lincoln heard her stockinged feet on bare planks, and the soft swishing sounds of skirt and petticoats as Billie changed. He remembered that Lucy had packed freshly ironed range pants and his canvas jacket. He would feel better in them than in the tight fit of his Sunday suit. Taking these outside to the stall, as a matter of proper modesty, he changed in the dark. When he returned, Billie stood in the lantern light, looking like a small boy in Beasley's turned-up pants and loose tucked-in shirt.

'They swallow me! But they'll be better to ride in than my suit.'

He nodded approval. 'The saddle horse will act better, too. Skirts worry a horse. You better wear the coat when you start, it'll be chilly till the sun gets up.'

He methodically folded his train clothes. He

stuffed them into his valise. Billie, simultaneously, was matching his action by packing her own suit, and trying to press in the new hat, without crushing it too much. The thought formed, as he noticed this, that they both were putting away old parts of their lives, something once important, no longer of use. The past was being packed away for a while, in favor of the present which was all that counted. Billie murmured, 'Now you look more like the Odessa country, the way I had pictured it.'

'How did you picture it?'

'I don't know. Untamed, I guess, but something I would like better than what I saw every night in the saloons.'

He flicked a glance to her. She met it solidly. Her hands went still on the bag fastenings. He saw something like misty blue velvet shine back the light reflections from her eyes. Her lips were poised between a smile, or a cry, he couldn't tell which, above the white flesh and lace edges revealed from the open collar of Beasley's dark shirt. His mouth felt dry and his fingers fumbled. When he heard her movements of getting into her blankets he blew out the lantern flame.

His first sound sleep came quickly, and later broke into full wakefulness as if his name had been called or a dog had growled somewhere at an intruder. Beasley's jumpy snoring, and the night wind's play with a loose board of the shed were the only sounds he could fix. The one high window made a faint gray square in the darkness, where moonlight seeped in enough to drape the hay bales and Beasley's blanket.

'Lincoln!'

He knew that this was the same whispered sound that had broken his slumber.

'Yes?'

'I can't sleep.'

'What's the trouble?'

Her murmur floated to him on the small wings of timidity. 'Will you come over here, Lincoln? It would be easier to talk.'

He got up and stepped across Beasley and went to where her blanket-wrapped form showed dimly on the floor.

'You can sit on the edge of my pallet.' She raised herself, supporting her head on her hand, edging back to make a space for him. 'Lincoln, what if they catch me starting to ride away? That would be terrible, for all of us, wouldn't it? I keep thinking of the old one, Uncle Dock. The way he looked at me.' She groped impulsively, closing cold fingers over the back of his hand, as if hunting strength against her fears. 'I can't tell you what he said to me before you came into the room tonight.'

'You'll make it, all right,' he told her, wanting to put down her worries. 'You'll get away, if I have to hold a gun on them. You ought to try to sleep now.'

'I will always wonder—about you.' She twisted, peering up to him. 'Whether you got away all right, I mean. And what became of you. If we both get to Fort Worth, will I see you again?'

'Might be we'd run into one another.' He meant to whisper it, but the words came out hoarse. He was newly aware of her physical nearness.

She was silent for a moment. 'In a place like this,' she said hesitantly, 'with all that's happened to us, it seems hard to remember that there is—anybody else, anywhere.'

It did. The plank walls of the shed, with their cracks making lacy vines of light where the moon rays squeezed through, closed in the only world existing. The rest was dissolved into nothing out there, by the wind and distances and oceans of mesquites dimming out to all horizons. He said, 'Things happened pretty fast today. I guess it will all fall back into shape, though, once we buckle up this business and find our footing again.'

'Lincoln, tell me how you were in with these people once. You're nothing like *them*! Or had you rather not talk about it?'

Lucy and the children seemed far away now. His Odessa life and his obligations were fragments of far-off misty spaces. Billie's fingers had been withdrawn from his hand, but her face and hair were so near he could have touched them by reaching only a few inches. He told her, then, how he was sent to live with Uncle Dock when he was orphaned as a small boy, and found himself entangled with a rowdy family of stagecoach and bank robbers.

'He has a hide-out place below Nuevo Laredo. His own domain, down there. He's the great kingpin, like a buffalo bull lording it over a herd. It took a lot of money, more than his ranch could make even working Mexican peons. The bunch came over to Texas every so often for a big holdup or robbery. The outsiders, the bad ones that would join up from time to time, they were always afraid of him, and of his kinfolks. The Tobins were a clannish bunch. He started me riding with them on some of the jobs. I hated them all, because my mother had married and left the family when she was young, and she was different from these.'

'Were you never in danger of being captured?'

'More than once,' he said numbly. 'Some were captured and some of them got killed or just disappeared. There were always new ones coming and going. The bunch is all new to me now. Except Uncle Dock and Claude. But word began to get out about me. I was seen a few places, and there was talk about the kid bandit with the Tobin gang. The law had my description, because I saw the reward circulars about the Tobins and they described me even better than Dock or the others. The most I ever did was to wait outside a place and hold their horses, and there wasn't one minute in those years that I wasn't scared to death, of the law and the gang and what I saw them do. All the time I planned on how to get away. It took a long time. When I did run for it, I went as far as I could, and I've been ever since trying to make a different life for myself. Now, that's the way it has been, Billie. This is the first time I've come east in ten years. Turns out this was a mistake.'

As he had talked, with the old scenes reborn in his memory, her hand had come to rest on his again. Billie said, 'I think a woman has made a lot of difference in you. I gather you married someone out there and she has helped you turn into—something different from the way you started.'

His thoughts scaled the shed walls and the mesquite horizons. How could he put it into words, how much Lucy had done?

When he did not speak, Billie murmured, 'I should not have sent your thoughts so far away.'

He had not gone so far, in one part of his consciousness. 'Maybe it was a good thing you did.'

She whispered, 'Why?'

His arm moved without his willing it. His fingers lightly brushed her hair in a fleeting stroke. 'You're a pretty woman, Billie.'

'You can't see me.'

'I know you're there, and what you look like.'

139

'I couldn't look like very much in these clothes of Sam's.'

'Not the clothes I'm talking about.'

After a moment, she murmured so softly that the words were nearly lost against the surge of his blood in his ears. 'Aren't you cold there, Lincoln?'

In the same instant, the crunch of a booted foot sounded heavily outside the door. A hard fist smashed against the wood, and the door flew open. Lincoln twisted toward it as Billie gasped and raised herself upright. The doorway framed a towering shadow filling the gray light of the opening, and he knew that Dock Tobin stood there searching for them in the darkness.

'Where's the woman, Link?' The old man's voice sawed across the silence like a jagged blade. 'She ought to be sleepin' up at the house. Dirty shed like this is no place to bed a woman.' The floor planks gave with Dock's measured stalk into the room.

Lincoln thought of his gun belt in his bedroll across the hay. The big shadow took form, peering over to their corner, and Billie's hands locked on his arm, holding him, and he caught the reek of whisky.

'Say, do I see you two over there?' Dock's voice wavered, pitched lower. He moved unsteadily around the bales.

Lincoln pressed Billie down with a hard shove to her shoulders and in the same motion

140

he squirmed under the covering blanket, until he was stretched full against her. He sought her face with his hand and pressed a finger against her lips.

'Yeah, we're here, Uncle.'

Dock came on, until his form towered over the pallet. He bent, spreading the whisky smell.

'Well, I be damn, Link!' The coughing laugh came out triumphantly.

Lincoln said, 'You go on back to the house. We're all right out here.'

'I'll say you are, boy! I was going to give her my bed—those fools ought not to have put a lady out in a cow shed like this. Woke up and got to thinking about that. Lady needs a bed.'

'She'll stay here.'

Dock stood above them for a long moment, his shadow swaying. He chuckled low in his chest and turned away. 'You've sure growed up, boy. You and Claude and me'll put some life in this crowd. We'll make the biggest haul we ever made, and you and the girl can have the time of your life when we get back to Nuevo Laredo.' Dock lumbered out the door. A small form bounded from the floor. Beasley's bare feet padded across, and he cautiously closed the door.

'I heard all that!' Beasley hissed. 'You want to get us killed?'

Lincoln stood, then stooped to lightly tuck the blanket covering back into place against Billie's rigid body.

141

'Don't panic, Beasley. He's gone and nobody's hurt.' He looked down at Billie's outline in the blankets, almost able to see her white features in the darkness. 'I didn't know of any other way to handle him,' he said gently. 'I knew *that* was the one most likely way.'

He went back to his blankets and wrapped himself in them, telling Beasley to quit his chattering. He nursed the butt of his .45 in his hand and closed his eyes, but for a long time sleep would not come.

CHAPTER TEN

The horses bunched and drifted around the pen in a circle, hugging the fence, and making more noise than Lincoln liked, but they calmed down after he threw the loop over the tail-ender which he thought would be a gentle one. He saddled, and when he crawled back through the feed gate the three of them stood unspeaking for a moment and their nervousness hung over the room like a sickness.

'I think you better carry this.' He pushed Beasley's little revolver into the coat pocket.

Beasley muttered, 'I sure hope you make it, Billie.'

She tried to show a smile to them. 'I feel like I'm up for my closing number on a rough

142

Saturday night.'

Beasley tried, too, shakily jaunty. 'Yeah, time for the Brown Brindle Bull.'

Her glance held on Lincoln. 'You never did hear my song, did you—about the cowboy and the girl and the brown brindle bull?'

'No, I guess not. Why?' He was wondering if a lookout might still be standing watch in the chilly dawn.

'Something has reminded me of it.'

'Well, you've got a real pretty voice, Billie.'

'In the song, the cowboy can hardly notice the girl for being so occupied with his new brown brindle bull.'

He said, 'Maybe I'll hear it sometime—remember to keep the shed between you and the house till you get in the brush.'

She raised her arms slightly to look down at her garb. 'Wouldn't I be a sight coming on the stage like this?' She did a small mocking step, thinly singing:

'The cowhand took the pretty lil gal
Ridin' when the moon was full—
She talked of love but all he would do
Was brag on his brown brindle bull.'

Her voice quavered at the end. They all knew the time had come and no amount of acting could change it.

Lincoln said, 'We'll go now. If they're all in the house, I'll not come out again.' He

143

hesitated. 'Good-by, Billie.'

'Good-by, Lincoln—Sam.' Then: 'See you in Fort Worth sometime.'

He and Beasley walked up the path through the broomweeds. The rocky spine of Ghost Ridge bared itself to daylight. Neither of them spoke until they were nearly at the house. Beasley murmured, 'That was my best suit.'

Billie had looked like a child playing dress up in Beasley's clothes with the turned-back sleeves and pants legs. *A mighty small package*, Lincoln thought, *a lot of country to get lost in*. He had wanted to tell her something reassuring, but it was too late now.

In the room, he was relieved to find Ponch Izaguirre and Coaley Scull. A skillet banging in the kitchen located Henny.

'Where's Uncle Dock?'

'Still in bed.' Ponch jerked a thumb toward the other room.

Coaley asked, 'The singer coming to breakfast?'

His first full look at Coaley this morning brought back the feel of a knife to his throat. He ignored the question, and Henny called, 'Grub's on!'

Dock came into the kitchen while they were eating. He was barefoot, in his pants, gun belt, and union suit. He spoke civilly to Lincoln and Beasley as he took the chair at the head of the plank table. 'Where's your woman, Link?'

'It's a little early for her.'

Dock beamed around the table. 'You-all ought to have seen what I saw last night.'

Ponch said, 'Tell us about it, Dock.'

The old man's expression changed. He smashed the table top with his fist so hard that all the plates bounced and Beasley strangled on a gulp of hot coffee. 'A damn water haul! You let that train guard run you off like a bunch of scared chickens. Twenty thousand dollars slipped through my fingers.' He took a long pull on a scalding tin cup and mumbled morosely, 'I wish I had my old bunch again. I wish I'd been there and had my eyesight. I'd have fixed that money guard with so much lead that it would look like train wheels had run over him. It's not like it used to be, Link. It's hard times we been having at the place. We got to have money before we go home.'

Ponch and Coaley had nothing to say to this, but Henny remarked, 'Well, why don't we try Byrd's Store? We been talking about it off and on for a year.'

'Claude will know,' Dock mumbled. 'Claude and Lincoln can plan it.'

Lincoln heard the talk vaguely, his mind at the corral and his ears unconsciously strained for sound of her horse. She would be started by now.

Ponch aimed his fork at Beasley. 'He staying with us?'

Lincoln said shortly, 'Yeah, he's staying.'

'We can always use another good man,'

Dock said.

'I got a pretty sore ankle,' said Beasley. 'Doubt if I'd be much help.'

Coaley got up. 'I wasn't very hungry. I'll go down to the corral and feed the horses.'

'Horses, hell!' Henny said.

Dock mumbled, 'Now don't you be bothering Link's girl.'

Coaley grinned, pleased, drawing up his thick shoulders. 'Never even thought of that. Cousin's wearing his six-gun this morning. Reckon it would be as much as man's life is worth to fool around his gal.'

Coaley roughly shoved at Henny's head, mussing his thin hair, and agiley jumped back when Henny slashed at him with a fork. He brushed the scattering of Henny's eggs off his suede jacket and chanted tunelessly:

'She said, Just look at the stars
They're so pretty tonight
I feel all fluttery and afire—
He said, I'm buildin' up a herd
With a brand all my own, me and
My far-ranging sire.'

Lincoln watched him swagger out of the room, knowing that in a matter of minutes Coaley would find that Billie was gone. The front door slammed behind Coaley. Lincoln pushed back and planted both palms flat on the table. 'I've got something to say to you. I'll run
146

it by once and that's all. You listen to this, Uncle. Nobody ever held out on a Tobin and kept his health, and the Tobins weren't the stripe that ever tried to hold out on each other. There was a valise down there that had a money belt in it. That money was mine and it's missing. It wasn't enough to be very much, split up. I guess somebody decided he'd help himself to the whole works. That means one of you two gents or Coaley. I want that money back.'

Dock hoisted his head and hung a blank stare on Ponch who twisted uneasily.

'Not me, Dock!'

'You're just the lard-bellied greaser that would try it. I'll cut your guts out, Ponch.'

Ponch twisted his bulldog head to pull Henny into it. Henny snarled, 'Don't look at me!'

Ponch's glare fell on Beasley. 'I bet there's your thief. That little tamale done it.'

Beasley began to sputter, but Lincoln cut it off. 'The man that got it can save himself from bad trouble if the money shows up in my valise again before noon.'

He left them, walked into the other room, and Beasley made haste to follow. 'Hell, Jones, don't make violence over that money. Play it easy with 'em—anything to keep 'em peaceable till we get out of here.'

'The time's passed for playing it easy. Billie's not on our hands now, Beasley. I've got to get my money back.'

147

'I wish you wouldn't talk like that.'

They heard fast walking outside. Coaley pounded in with his boots hammering. 'All right, mister!' he gritted. 'Where's she gone?'

The others were coming into the room and Dock demanded, 'Where's who gone?'

'The girl!' Coaley flung it at them. 'There's a horse missing and the girl's vamoosed.'

The old man turned on Lincoln. 'Did you send that girl off?'

'I guess she pulled out on her own.'

'She can make us a lot of trouble if she gets to the law,' Henny told Dock.

'I want that woman brought back! Ponch and Coaley—straddle your horses!'

They would run her down all right. Like eager hounds. But he would not let that happen. A fine recklessness lifted him. His tone stopped Ponch and Coaley. 'You're not going anywhere. The first one that touches that doorknob will never live to turn it.'

They locked their movements, to see what went with the force in the words. Lincoln held his Colt in his hand. Ponch looked long at the gun, Coaley resentfully at Lincoln's features, bright with invitation.

Inaction in the room strung out until his ears began to ring as if a metallic hum came with the shaft of sun rays flecking a million glints off the window.

Coaley spoke first, in the deceptive mildness of a man hiding a club from a dog he meant to whip. 'No call for gunplay.'

148

Dock's wild laugh shook the room. As if he had forgotten, with his interest cascading off to cards of new promise, Dock chortled. 'By God, that's tellin' 'em, son! I see neither of 'em is anxious to touch that doorknob!' Lincoln felt it there again—the old man's unpredictable turn, coming solid between him and whatever Coaley and Ponch might have done. They drew back from the door.

Ponch mumbled, 'She'll go to the law, Dock. Soon as she gets a chance.'

'You see the way Link upped with that gun?' Dock demanded. 'Quick as a cat, that boy. Taught him myself.'

Henny grumbled. 'I'd like to know who fixed it for her to ride off? She couldn't 'a roped a mount and saddled by herself, way she looked to me.'

As if the situation needed some outlet that would salve his pride, and one that nobody would object to his working over, Coaley advanced on Beasley. He reached a heavy hand, twisting it into Beasley's coat front. Beasley appeared to shrink to half size as Coaley vigorously shook him. 'You're the one that schemed it up. I ought to take you down and cut your ears off!'

Beasley threw an agonizing plea to Lincoln with the whites of his eyes. Ponch leaned across Coaley and twisted Beasley's nose. The gambler squealed in pain. Dock chuckled.

Coaley swung Beasley around with a

powerful twist on his arm. 'You sent the girl to bring the law on us, didn't you?'

Beasley trod on tiptoes against the twisting Coaley was giving him. 'I swear I didn't! Swear to God—it wasn't me!'

Coaley twisted harder, grinning with his lips sucked over his teeth, his eyes burning glassy-black. 'Who did it, then? Tell us who did, or I'll unbuckle this arm and knock you down with it!'

Beasley moaned. He twisted his sweat-beaded face and jabbed his free hand in pointing motions across his straining body. 'He did! Jones did! He saddled a horse and sent her off, so help me!'

Coaley gave a final twist and shoved Beasley reeling across the floor.

Coaley and Ponch turned triumphantly toward Dock Tobin. They had brought the issue back, now. Lincoln saw through the bullying of Beasley. They knew the tricky means of herding Uncle Dock's peculiar mind into the chute they wanted.

Dock moved barefooted upon Lincoln, so close he could blow his bacon-and-old-whisky breath into Lincoln's nostrils. 'Who told you she could leave?'

He could tug of war with Dock's mind, too.

He traded breakfast breaths with Dock, not leaning away. He noticed how he could look down at Dock, by an inch, and remembered how tall the old man had once seemed to him.

150

'Coaley is doing a lot of talking,' Lincoln said distinctly. 'Like a man that's just stolen six hundred dollars out of a valise and wants everybody to forget it happened, so he talks about the girl.'

Coaley flipped his watch leather faster. 'What're you gabbin' about now?'

'I remember once, Uncle—a fellow you called Bo Jeeter held out some money on the bunch after that job in Laredo and when you caught Bo red-handed, you and Claude tied him to a rafter and whipped him with a bullwhip till he chewed up and swallowed a handful of federal currency. You said it was worth a hundred dollars to see that Bo got his fill. I wonder how Coaley would look eating a canvas money belt?'

'We sure did.' Dock nodded solemnly. He addressed the room. 'I made Bo Jeeter swaller a hundred dollars worth of paper. Coaley, how come you went through those bags? Where's that money?'

Coaley looked uneasy, and genuinely puzzled, Lincoln thought. But he couldn't tell about Coaley's looks. He was a good actor.

'What money you talking about?'

'The money that was in my valise.'

'You mean it's gone? It was in there last night—I told you. I just looked through some of those bags, in a hurry. I didn't take anything out of them.'

Henny said, 'Maybe the filly took it.'

151

Lincoln listened to the harangue in which all of them joined. This was something old and remembered, the eternal squabbling of the Tobin bunch in the monotonous days of their hide-outs after a robbery. He watched their fever rise as they traded curses and accusations, running the blame among Coaley, Ponch, and Henny like passing around something that smelled and nobody wanted to hold. And this was fine, for every minute of it meant Billie was riding farther away, and that chance of pursuit grew less while they argued over the identity of the thief among the thieves. Beasley's head hung, not meeting Lincoln's glance at him after the way he had been tortured into blaming Lincoln for Billie's escape. He looked miserable.

Then Dock Tobin's mind remembered. He roared, 'I told somebody to go find the girl!'

Coaley headed for the door. 'You sure did! You stay here, Ponch, I'll find her myself.' Lincoln had holstered his gun. Coaley, looking at Ponch, made a sign, and Ponch responded with his six-gun springing to his fist. Coaley hitched his belt and said airily, 'I may be late getting back.'

Henny bleakly scowled and grunted to Ponch, 'Let Jones have it if he argues. That woman could hang us all.'

The gun in Ponch's hand didn't matter. Nothing like that was going to happen unless Dock gave the word. He could try one more time in this delicate game of juggling Uncle

152

Dock's mind.

'If he gets out of the house, Uncle, he'll hide that money he stole from the rest of you. You knew how to handle Bo Jeeter. I think Cousin Coaley needs the same lesson.'

The jauntiness drained out of Coaley. He stopped and looked back uneasily at Dock. 'By God, I'm getting tired of him saying that! I didn't take the money.' His fear of the old man draped each word.

Like the changing shadows of morning, Billie's escape again melted aside and the bigger crime took its place in the room. Now Dock's six-gun came up in his gnarled fingers. Seeing that, Ponch immediately holstered his own. Dock's bare feet padded across. 'You want to eat that money, Coaley?'

'Search me! Go on, search me!' Coaley's voice cracked. 'You think I got it? See if I got it on me!'

Dock's frame slackened. 'He ain't got it.'

Lincoln drawled, 'I'll call his bluff. I'll search him.' This was gaining minutes, and enough of them strung out was distance in the mesquites.

Coaley snarled, 'You ain't got the guts enough to try it!'

'Well, now, we're all in the family. Let's just take a look at one another's guts. Shuck off your gun belt.'

Savagely, Coaley's hands tore into the buckle, ripped the belt open, and flung it with his holstered gun to a chair. Lincoln slowly

153

removed his own belt and gun, handing them to Dock. Ponch pulled a chair out of the way with a quick grab, and Henny began muttering under his breath. Beasley tried to blot himself out against a wall. The door Coaley had opened lazed back and forth on old hinges that squeaked like mice nests. Time moved back to last night, with this big-muscled and mean-streaked animal probing a knife to his throat. Lincoln listed the scheming orbs too small in the oversized olive face, sideburns too long, chest too wide, too much badness bred into him like both sides had concentrated on it. His memory registered two distinctive thuds on the bare boards that nothing on earth could make but a woman dropping her shoes. *Keep riding, Billie, I'll occupy him for a while.*

Uncle Dock, now, as before, liked a roughhouse. It could last as long as Uncle Dock enjoyed it or until he switched his mind to something else.

'You were giving the order last night, Coaley. I give you the same one now.' Lincoln checked Ponch and Henny from the corner of his eyes, the guns, the position of Coaley's feet. 'Show us the money. *Take off your clothes!*'

He saw that Coaley looked cunning and confident, getting his muscles and his intentions pulled together. The fight would be nothing extra bad, by Odessa standards of things to contend with. A man was always having to do some mean job with his hands and

154

scramble like hell all the time just to keep the country from overpowering him. It would even be all right if Coaley pulled his spring blade. Then he might kill Coaley somehow, and get it over. He studied Coaley in the swollen moment of showdown between them, as he would size up a killer stallion that had to be bridled.

Coaley fixed his fists, set his weight. He sneered. 'Gentleman from Odessa, huh? That means a *sonofabitch*!'

Lincoln nodded. 'That's what the Indians say. That's the Comanche language. We showed 'em a new way to use a scalpin' knife.'

Then Coaley charged him.

It seemed to him Coaley had been exposing for an hour what he meant to do first, the *cabrón* style of Coahuila fighters with big shoulders and hard heads, the low-rushing butt of a head into a man's stomach that would smash his intestines at once and end the fight before it started. *Coaley's not smart enough to fight good*, he thought; and the way you do it for the *cabrón* is coil your middle out of the way as a tall man can do and hardly change tracks, so you can keep your target. Then you see if you can break the man's backbone while he's bulling by, bent low and spine taut, by coming down on it with a fist like swinging an ax to firewood.

Coaley smacked face-first to the floor and the room shook. Lincoln waited, interested to see if Coaley could get up, for usually nobody

155

did for a while, and when they did they stepped high in all directions like a Kiowa beginning to dance and tried to hold their backbone with both hands as if their bodies might separate into two pieces.

Coaley got up sleepily and did the high, agonizing steps of a Kiowa. He tried to hold his backbone in his hands. The noise like the door hinges, but louder, was Coaley crying. They all stared with interest at the unusual contortions in Coaley's mouth and legs. When his steps died down he got his hands around in front and came at Lincoln, tears showing, and this time he did not butt. He threw arms and fists ahead of him on a tide of curses, the same one over and over. His weight and power carried Lincoln against a wall. One head blow hurt, not with sharp pain, but enough to warn what Coaley's strength could do. He stretched his angular legs and arms to get at Coaley from everywhere, as if chousing a wild steer into a gate. He hacked at Coaley with bony wrists, flinty knuckles, high-jabbing knees, and slapped him twice with his open hand because Coaley's full olive cheeks invited that and it popped his eyes with rage.

So Coaley withdrew a few steps, attending to the blood on his face with both sleeves. He made a dazed turn of his head toward his six-gun on the chair against the wall. Seeing this, Lincoln leaned far out to knock his head back around. Coaley made a half-sobbing bellow, lowered his head, and plowed blindly in with his big fingers digging for Lincoln's eyes. One made it, stabbing hot as a branding iron. They grappled, slipped, and stumbled as their boots skidded, and Dock crept back and forth to keep out of the way, softly hitting one palm with his fist in rhythmic time beat. Lincoln had to give way to the next rush. Coaley was hard to put down. Solid, big, and heavy. Fists like anvils. Lincoln tasted blood and spat it aside. Coaley swung in great desperate blows, and in between them he moaned and tried to grab at his back. Then Lincoln feinted for his head with his left fist, Coaley's guard flew up, Lincoln started his right fist from three feet behind him, burying it to the wrist in the exposed stomach.

Coaley clattered on his heels all the way across the room and sat down against the wall. His eyes roamed wildly to everybody begging help for his lungs. When his first air rattled in through his stretched mouth it sounded like the noise of a wild cow running through dry-creek gravel. Lincoln stood over Coaley. He stooped, tugged, dumped Coaley around, and came up with his embroidered suede jacket. He handed it to Henny.

'Your shirt now. *Undress!*'

Coaley swarmed him at the knees and they fought all over the room. Beasley sounded like the drone of a beehive. 'That's enough, that's enough!'

In the tangle Lincoln ripped Coaley's shirt open, the buttons flying. Coaley up-kicked at his groin. Lincoln arched in. The boot toe grazed past. He caught it, twisting with hands that had bulldogged and branded three-year-olds days on end. When Coaley bumped the floor, Lincoln kept the foot-hold twist and plowed the planks with him until he went inert.

Dock said, 'Fetch up some whisky, Henny!'

Lincoln finished with Coaley's shirt, tearing off the last pieces. He put too much attention to that. Coaley swung his fist out of nowhere, knocking Lincoln backward.

On their feet again, Coaley crouched, naked to the waist, except for a piece of tattered sleeve that had not come off. Blood dripped steadily from his mouth and nose, running down the muscle mounds of his body. Lincoln bored in again.

'*Undress, Coaley!* Ain't that what you kept telling her?'

Coaley backed away, circling, Lincoln following. Coaley plunged in, swinging his fists. Lincoln threw fist for fist until each rocked the other way. Back a distance now, Coaley turned his side. His hand moved as he stooped. Lincoln heard the spring click. The blade flew open.

Beasley moaned, 'No. No. No—'

The thin white edge waved back and forth, razor-bright. Coaley's lips drew up over his bloody top teeth, his hand floating the blade

158

back and forth like the weaving head of a coiled copperhead. Coaley kept coming. Lincoln circled backward, eyes following the knife motions. Didn't know whether Coaley would slice, when he was ready, or stab. A slicer was harder to handle than a stabber. One more step. Now—the chair.

Coaley plunged, showing himself a slicer. But the rawhide-bottomed chair met him. The first slash struck the extended pine legs as Lincoln parried it against the knife. Coaley faked an up slash, then a low, but the chair legs punched his hand each time.

Lincoln backed slowly, Coaley coming. Against the door edge, then through the opening as the door swung, backward into the sunlight, into the weedy yard. Over Coaley's head he saw them trooping after, the four bunched men. Their necks craned to watch the knife and the chair.

The chair play was too tantalizing. Making a fool of Coaley, so now he hurried too much. Lincoln saw the big try coming in Coaley's eyes. When he charged into the chair, grabbing at it, Lincoln gave him the chair from a loose grip. Coaley's jerk on it, and the unexpected slack, threw him off balance.

Whirling sidewise at the same instant, Lincoln's fingers locked around Coaley's wrists fast as a steel trap closing. As Coaley unglued his left hand from the chair rounds, his knife hand was no longer his, but a red-hot ball of pain somewhere back between his shoulder blades. Lincoln kept him circling so that his head never came up again.

'You shouldn't have pulled the knife.'

With his head bent to his knees from the pain vise that was breaking his fingers off behind him, Coaley made one childish try, nudging his blood-smeared mouth against the hard thigh at his face and sinking his teeth into cloth and muscle.

Doesn't hurt much, Lincoln thought, *if he's not poison.* He jerked his leg, kicked the knife into the weeds, and turned Coaley around. He aimed for Coaley's chin, and knocked him in a backward stumble, halfway to the pin oak tree. After him fast. He was tiring a little. This was about enough. He uncoiled everything into a smash with the left sideburn his target. Then he took his time. Coaley saw nothing, knew nothing. With Coaley stumbling drunkenly back, he followed, hitting and following, until his breath came hard and his eyes blurred with exertion.

When Coaley fell, it was on the fresh clods of Alcutt's grave.

Lincoln got down in the dirt with him. Coaley tried a blind swing at Lincoln's head. Lincoln angered unreasonably because Coaley still fought, and methodically adjusted his long fingers around Coaley's thick throat. Kicking and flopping did Coaley no good. Nothing to fight with when dying.

160

Dock and Ponch and Henny, with Beasley peering from behind, watched Coaley's eyes swell, heard his lungs labor, his throat rattle, and remarked his limpness when it came.

Lincoln looked up at them through the sweat. 'That's like going under once.' He could hardly hear himself. 'Like drowning, going under the first time.' He studied Coaley, then bent and blew against Coaley's nose. He crawled down and went to work on Coaley's boots, pulled them off, then the socks, dropped Coaley's feet, moved over to take off his pants. He struggled with this, for Coaley was dead weight. When Coaley lay on Alcutt's flat grave top in only his drawers, he revived. Lincoln waited until Coaley was full conscious.

He threw Coaley's pants aside to the weeds and stumbled around to Coaley's head. Kneeling, he fitted his fingers around Coaley's thick throat again. Coaley flopped every way like a perch on the bank, and tore at Lincoln's hands, but it made no difference. He drowned again.

Ponch muttered, 'Godamighty!'

Uncle Dock nudged the man nearest to him, not looking away from it. 'Watch this—you ever see anything like this?'

'It's like going under the second time,' Lincoln said. He paid close attention. It was something you had to time just right. He took his hands from Coaley's neck.

He got up and tugged off Coaley's drawers.

A red ant had already come up on Coaley's stomach and Lincoln flicked it away with a finger thump.

He looked down at Coaley, who was beginning to make rusty breathing sounds again. He had told Billie that Coaley deserved killing twice, for last night.

Dock kept staring down, fascinated. 'You-all notice how he looks like he might of come up from *inside* that grave?'

Lincoln dropped the long-legged ribbed drawers over Coaley's nakedness. Coaley had been stripped and there was no money belt on him.

Dock boomed, 'I said bring the whisky, Henny!' He found the paralyzed Beasley with searching eyes. 'Ain't the Tobins a bunch, though, feller?'

Lincoln looked at the sun. It hadn't come up any higher, seemed like. This had all happened in no time, he guessed, though it had seemed to last all morning. But she would be quite a way off by now, and nobody was going to chase her down.

He said, 'He didn't have the money on him, after all, did he?'

Ponch and Henny drew out of his way. Coaley stirred and began his first efforts to sit up. He didn't look very good there to Lincoln, and likely not to the others. They all turned their backs on Coaley Scull, with Alcutt under

162

him and Buckshot Withers on the other side of the pin oak, and followed Lincoln to the house.

CHAPTER ELEVEN

The sun worked high and brassy to warm up the green land of deformed mesquites and red rock upthrusts. Preparations were made to travel just as soon as Claude arrived. With his hurts washed at the windmill trough, Lincoln worked with the others, resigned to the necessity of playing it out, of making himself one of them.

Nobody would ever know how close he had come to putting his fingers a third time to Coaley's throat and finishing him. He didn't know, himself, why he had not. Coaley had intended to rip the life out of him.

Beasley hovered about, but said little after his first anxious questions were cut off. Coaley mostly stayed out of sight during the day, nursing his hurts somewhere in the brush on lookout or on a hay bed in the shed. Henny and Ponch went at things like two old ranch hands with jobs to do and with Lincoln the foreman to consult and satisfy.

All the mounts were fed and watered. As much of Alcutt's feed was loaded as the big wagons afforded space. The water kegs were filled at the windmill. The Tobins had a saddle horse apiece and four extra mounts, all of them

163

good horseflesh of Mexican mustang blood, the best there was for endurance. Dock ordered Alcutt's three scissortails added to the spares, to be trailed from the wagons on lead ropes. Lincoln picked the best of the Tobin spares, a coffee-hued mustang with lively movements, and helped himself to Henny's saddle rig. Henny was to drive one wagon, Uncle Dock the other. The procession would drift south through a land in which there was small chance of being sighted. It was unsettled country, all the way to the Butterfield Trail and Byrd's Store. The Byrd's Store strike would be risky, but the store served as a stage-line bank and if they caught it with a money shipment on hand the pickings could be big.

Lincoln registered that Dock still traveled with signs of the old prosperity, even if his domain in Mexico was a crumbling outfit of bandit families and peon ranch hands. The two Studebaker wagons looked to be in good repair, the grub supply was ample, the bedrolls, armament, and other travel gear sufficient. Flight from Texas by wagon would not be his idea of a quick getaway to the Rio Grande, but there had been the problem of Uncle Dock's sight handicap in riding horseback. There was also merit in their idea that two meandering wagons sighted by any transient brush rider would suggest only a nester outfit on the move, not as suspicious as mounted men riding through a wild country.

Nobody would consider sending word to the rangers if they merely sighted two covered wagons plodding along. Ponch offered the additional explanation that if anyone got nosy, and rode up to look them over, a man or two under the wagon covers with rifles ready could knock 'em off easy while their attention was held by the others.

Lincoln nodded. 'We carry our own ambush with us.'

'We took care of a *bastardo* that way, comin' up,' Ponch related. 'Henny had a bead on him from under the wagon cover and Claude decided this bird was thinkin' too much, lookin' us over. He gave the sign and Henny blew the feller clear off his horse, then Dock shot the horse. Less somebody spotted us crossin' the Rio the first night, ain't nobody knows we're up here. Just the *familia*.'

'What does that amount to now, down there?' Lincoln felt an irrepressible pull of old interest. He visualized the big adobe headquarters house in the Madre foothills, and the cluster of huts around it, the corrals, pastures, and fields.

Ponch proclaimed that they were mostly lazy bastards living off Dock's herds and raid loot, a settlement given to long siestas in the shade, *tequila* flowing in the evenings, and women enough for everybody, counting the Mexican women and the Tobin second cousins and in-laws. It was a good life down there,

Ponch assured. Link would be glad he'd come back. Shame he hadn't elected to bring the singing woman with him. Only when the money got scarce did they have to exert themselves. It developed that Henny was Dock's brother-in-law by one of Dock's wives, that Ponch's wife was Dock's cousin through a complicated Mexican lineage and that Coaley Scull was *her* son of an illegitimate birth, fathered by a man who had ridden with the bunch and had been killed in a saloon fight at Villa Acuna. Of the old bunch, the Berring brothers, whom Lincoln remembered, had just vanished, somewhere up in the Indian Nation. Dock himself had killed Latigo Gonzales; Claude had killed Kansas Bill when Kansas had pulled a gun on Dock, and the law had nabbed Mev Trout on the Texas side and sent him to the pen for his part in the Uvalde holdup. Lincoln remembered Trout, like he remembered Claude, as a cold-blooded killer. Claude was Dock's nephew, but Lincoln had never thought of him as his own cousin, for he was ten years older and already a dedicated bad man when the well-meaning neighbors in far-off Nacogdoches had shipped the orphaned Jones lad south to Laredo to make his home with ranching relatives.

These things he heard from Ponch piecemeal as they fed and watered the mounts, tied on the lead ropes, and stowed the equipment in the wagons. At straight-up noon, Henny went to the house with an armful of stove wood to heat up some victuals, and Dock showed up to inspect the horses and wagon loading. Apparently satisfied, he then turned toward the shed and bellowed, '*Coaley!*'

Coaley limped out of the shed in a minute, his face showing cuts and pulpy bruises. Sometime during the morning he had regained his gun belt and had added another one, the two crisscrossing and swinging holstered guns on both his legs, the way Claude always had worn his. Claude kept his holsters thonged down, for he was the quickest-draw man in the country, they all had said, and he was never going to be taken alive by any Texas Ranger or anybody else. Coaley stalked past without glancing at them as Uncle Dock told him to go ride to the top of Ghost Ridge before he ate and take a gander over the country.

When Beasley had a chance to speak to Lincoln aside, he mumbled, 'I hope you ain't mad at me, Jones. I couldn't help it.'

'Couldn't help what?'

'Sayin' you was the one that sent Billie.' Beasley's eye-balls circled and his mouth corners jumped. 'He was twisting my arm off.'

Lincoln had no time to waste on Beasley. Beasley had begun to look to him like an outsider, the same as he looked to the others. 'Just get to hell out of the way, Beasley,' he said gruffly. 'Don't bother me now.'

But Beasley hovered close like a cur

dragging his tail. 'That sure was some fight, Jones. By gaddly, you sure cleaned his plow! I never saw nothing like it before in all my life.'

Lincoln backed him off with a hard look, but Beasley was around again in a minute. 'When we gonna leave 'em, Jones? Can't we get away before that Claude feller comes?'

Lincoln paused to stare down at the gambler's misery. 'I'll tell you one thing you can do, Beasley—see if you can find out which one's got my money. Keep your eyes peeled for that. I can't watch them all. See if you can figure it out—you're crook enough to know the signs.'

Beasley looked so hurt that Lincoln regretted his bitterness but he was in an ugly frame of mind. He said, 'If you want to do something to help me, that's what you can do. It's not much but I guess there's not much guts to you anyhow, and I wouldn't look for you to do anything that took any.'

Beasley's rabbity eyes halted their evasive sliding. His mouth tightened. He looked drawn and years older than yesterday. 'I admit I ain't been much help.' His jaw knotted in a way Lincoln had not seen before, and his shoulders squared a little. 'Been run over a long time. Feller gets tired of it. I'll help you find that money, Jones. Anything else you want me to do, you say so.'

Beasley turned and purposefully headed for the house without waiting for Lincoln to lead

168

the way.

The early afternoon wore along, with everything in readiness for pulling out at sundown. The start would be made with night traveling. Sunup was calculated to find them far south of the tracks. They would make a day hole-up there, unless Claude decided they should put more miles behind them. Claude would bring the full story of how things stood at the Crosscut end.

As time approached for him to ride in, an atmosphere of uneasiness settled on Ghost Ridge. Everyone knew Claude would be in a state because the holdup had failed. Lincoln sensed the new tension. The bright, silent afternoon had the feeling of hidden menace, reminding him of the times when some unexplained inner sense had warned of Indian trouble hours before an attack actually came.

Coaley Scull had not come back from his scouting ride to the top of the ridge. Henny said that he was likely up there sulkin' or sleepin' and he did not save food from the noon meal, but went ahead to pack his utensils.

Lincoln walked down to the corral. Sam Beasley came along after a while and sat with his back to a wagon wheel, on the shady side, with his hat over his eyes, dozing or worrying. All the saddles straddled the top pole of the fence in a parade, with the bridles and blankets on the rails under them. Everything was ready and waiting for Claude.

He went into the pen, took a lariat from a saddle, and threw a loop over his chosen mount, which reared a couple of times, then followed him livelily to the windmill trough. It was time for all the *remuda* to be watered again, but he was interested only in the one he had picked for himself. The others could look after their own.

This done, he replaced the rope, the saddle reminding him of Billie Ellis's ride and starting a speculation on how she was making it.

From the front door of the shack, Henny came out and shaded his eyes in a long look toward the rock-crusted upthrusts of the distant ridge. This started Lincoln thinking that Coaley had been gone unduly long. It didn't seem natural that Coaley would skip a meal. He would be swaggering around again before long, and Lincoln considered with dull certainty that Coaley's pride was going to prod fresh trouble. He would have to watch Coaley asleep and awake. He was nobody to turn a back to, not after this morning. And in that moment, the hair up and down his neck prickled like a hundred crawling bugs. His breath shortened and a thin ringing started up in his ears. He made his hands keep working at what he was doing, fastening the rope coil back to the saddle, but his eyes worked everywhere from under his hatbrim.

He should have thought of it before. Coaley wouldn't have been up on the ridge all this time. Where was he?

Lincoln's back was toward the shed, a position he regretted immediately. He tried for a natural pace in the way he walked around to the gate, and out of the pen. A prickly-pear itch played between his shoulder blades. Where would Coaley likely be?

He hesitated briefly, making a sweeping glance to the mesquites, over to the shed corner, and toward the house. He could not place what it was that had flagged his notice. Ponch squatted against a wall at the house. Beasley still dozed beside a wagon. Neither of them looked at him. Yet something moved somewhere. He felt as tall and exposed as the windmill. A tumbleweed rolled into sight of his eye corner. Its motion jerked his head that way. His hand hovered at the gun belt.

Beasley stirred, stretched his arms, and stood. That movement by Beasley sent his glance to the wagon. Instantly, he caught the faint ripple of the faded wagon cover, a small bulge inside that moved the canvas wrong for the way the breeze played. Something moved in the shadowed gap between the cover edge and the wagon side.

He had not changed his steps nor his course. He saw the rifle barrel as it poked through the gap. Beasley stepped out, still stretching his arms, and Lincoln choked off a yell to him because that might have stampeded Beasley the wrong way.

But Beasley saw his expression, or heard a sound behind him. He whirled to face the short section of a rifle muzzle poking out. The sight of it must have exploded Beasley's mind into the desperation of doing something, anything. He lunged and grabbed at the rifle barrel that trained on Lincoln, and sounded a short, shrill bleat like a goat caught in a crevice.

The rifle barrel gave with his tug. Beasley had it with both hands, pulling and sawing. The muzzle came off Lincoln, and onto Beasley. The explosion from inside the cover made Beasley throw up his hands and stagger back. Lincoln's Colt roared twice, then a third time, as he triggered bullets to the bulge of his unseen target behind the cover. Beasley collapsed on the ground and the rifle hung half out of the wagon.

Lincoln went to Beasley, reloading as he moved. Ponch and Henny, and then Dock, headed down from the house.

A dark stain spread on Beasley's shirt. By the time he straightened Beasley out to make him a little more comfortable, and got his clothes open to examine the wound, somebody was up in the wagon, dragging something heavy toward the tailgate. He looked that way as Ponch hefted Coaley over to Dock and Henny. They stretched Coaley alongside the wheel, close to where Beasley lay.

Henny straightened. 'This one's dead. How about him?'

172

Beasley's eyes fluttered open, not jumpy now, only dull and staring. A light of recognition formed for Lincoln and dulled again. Beasley whispered, 'Am I hurt bad, Jones?'

Lincoln squatted close, looking at the hole in Beasley's white chest. 'You take it easy now.'

Beasley closed his eyes. His lips worked. Lincoln bent close to hear. 'By gaddly, I'm a man to have around, Jones. He might of shot you—'

Lincoln glanced blindly at Coaley Scull's still form and back to Beasley. 'You sure are—Sam.' He had such a dryness in his throat he had to clear it hard.

'I ain't ever had much guts—'

'You did fine.'

'You—tell—'em—about me in—Crosscut.' His words trailed off sleepily.

Lincoln said he would sure tell 'em about Sam Beasley, but Sam was dead by then.

Ponch muttered that Coaley had three slug holes in him. 'He asked for 'em. Been askin' for that all his life.' They all tromped the grass and looked at the dead pair, first at one, then the other, and up at the holes the .45 had made in the canvas.

'That's two to bury,' Dock said. He swung his head, pointing his sight around until he could see Lincoln better. 'What was all the shootin' about, boy?'

Lincoln looked out over the mesquites. The

173

horses in the pen had stiffened their ears and bunched at the west side. Somebody was coming. 'Coaley tried to ambush me from the wagon,' he said, thinking hard for some way he might have saved Beasley. 'This other one, Beasley—he grabbed the rifle. He got the bullet Coaley meant for me.'

Lincoln put a shoulder against the tailgate and made a smoke, listening. Dock and the others heard, too, and turned to watch the brush.

Ponch rubbed a heavy fist over his pulpy nose. 'Maybe that's Claude now.'

Dock Tobin spoke to Lincoln over his shoulder. 'You bury Coaley, boy. Him and that other feller. Up there where you buried Buckshot.'

'I'll bury Beasley,' Lincoln said. 'If you want Coaley buried, do it yourself. I've dug the grave for my last sonofabitch'.

Horses sounded in the brush. Henny pulled his gun. 'I reckon that's Claude. But be ready.'

They had spread out a little, guns in hands, when the three horses walked out of the scrub mesquites and into the clearing. Ponch said, 'There's Claude.'

Henny shaded his eyes against the sun. 'It's Claude, all right. And damned if he ain't brought Mev Trout with him. But who's the other little feller?'

Lincoln stared and all the blood seemed to drain out of his veins. The forlorn, white-faced rider in baggy clothes, on the horse trailing Claude and Mev Trout, was Billie Ellis.

CHAPTER TWELVE

Claude Tobin spared Lincoln little more notice than if they had parted an hour before. A stocky, sun-blackened man of thick muscles and aggressive movements, he came over now to make a scowling survey of things, moving Ponch and Henny out of his way with a hand gesture.

Trout drifted to one side and stood hipshot in his tight-fitting black garb like a thin raven aloofly watching a scene that privately amused him. Lincoln waited to see what Claude's reaction would be, noticing how the others waited, too.

Billie trudged around the men and timidly came close to his side. She averted her head after a quick look at the bodies on the ground.

'I did everything wrong,' she said in misery. 'I rode out of my way to head them off, never dreaming—'

'What you get for running out on me!' Lincoln rasped. He twisted his fist in the coat front, jerking her to him, and slapped her face on both sides and shoved her away. She caught her balance and stared openmouthed, but she was thinking fast, too, and came back, pressing

175

close to him, with her chin low in subjection.

'I won't run out on you again, Link. I'm sorry I got mad.'

'See that you don't.'

Ponch made an answer to Claude's impatient eye probing.

'Coaley shot this 'un and he shot him.' He deciphered by pointing.

'His name Beasley?'

'*Si*. He was on the train.'

'I know.'

Dock told Claude, 'That's Link Jones. He's come back to join us. He whipped hell out of Coaley this morning. Coaley tried to ambush him.'

'Uh-huh. Heard you was back.' Claude looked him over, as if calculating the changes. Then the wagons and the horses in the pen claimed his attention. 'We ready to travel?'

Lincoln glanced inquiringly at Billie. How much had she told Claude and Trout?

She said, 'They already knew.'

He asked sharply, not liking this, 'How was that, Claude?'

'In Crosscut. They got you tabbed as brainin' the train holdup.'

He searched Claude's face to see if he was lying. The truth was there, though, and it was like the ground had been jerked out from under his feet.

'That town marshal? He get it all added up?'

'Kincaid, yeah. They've doped it out that

176

Link Jones was on the train. Every lawman in the state is looking for you by now.' Claude motioned to Billie. 'Her, too.'

'Why her?'

'She and a gambler named Beasley left town on that train. None of you showed up again after the wood stop. They burned up the telegraph wires when the train got to Eskota. Everybody figured it out that you three were in cahoots with the bandits.'

'Kincaid remembered me?'

'After he got the news, he looked through some old reward posters. You haven't changed in looks much. He found out you'd come in on the stage from the west. The stage driver remembered, too. He was in Cottonwood that time we took over the town and says he never forgot the boy that rode with the bunch. Remember that? So he and Kincaid figured out Link Jones got on the train with his two chums to help pull the holdup.'

'You heard all that?'

'It was the talk around the saloons before we pulled out.'

In the silence that followed, Dock spoke to Trout. 'When did they let you out?'

Trout took a slow pull on his smoke. His washed-out eyes floated around the group. 'Couple of weeks ago.'

Dock rumbled, 'Well, we lost Coaley and got back Mev. Guess we won in the swap. Let's start rollin', boys. And don't none of you

177

monkey with the calico. She's Link's woman.'

Billie touch Lincoln's arm and murmured, 'How did it happen? Sam?'

'Coaley.'

His mind reeled with what Claude had said. The stage driver and Kincaid figuring it out. Telegraph reports going back about him and Beasley and Billie disappearing from the train. The law putting it all together. Reward posters going up once more for Link Jones.

Claude snapped, 'I don't like it.'

'I like it even less.'

'It ties the Tobins into that job. They could give us trouble toward the border.'

Claude took a few steps back and forth, threw a frowning glance at the bodies, and out at the low hang of the sun.

'Ponch, you and Henny haul these two out to a gully somewhere. Cover them up with rocks. Work fast. Mev, you remember how to hitch a team? Get the mules to these wagons.' He raked a glance over Lincoln, inquiringly across to Dock, and back again. 'You part of this outfit or not?'

He felt every Winchester in the hands of every trigger happy posse rider in the country trained on his back.

'Yeah, I'm in the outfit. What the hell do you think I came back for?'

Dock boomed, 'Link and you're gonna pull that Byrd's Store deal.'

Claude shrugged. 'Maybe.' He turned on

178

Ponch and Henny. 'I'm wantin' to know how you flopped on that train job. But first, get on with Coaley and this other one. We've got to move.' To Lincoln he said, 'While Trout hitches, we'll be saddlin' the mounts. You remember Mev?'

The flat stare in Trout's white sockets made a flicker of recognition. He wore a face pallor from the prison years, but his two tied-down black gun holsters looked natural. Lincoln said, 'Howdy, Trout.' Trout made a lazy finger motion of response.

Dock told Billie, 'You'll ride in my wagon, girl. All the way home to Mexico. Right with your Uncle Dock.'

Trout murmured, 'Dock ain't changed much.'

Lincoln managed to speak with Billie alone when the others moved on to the corral.

'What happened out there?'

'Oh, Lincoln, it was terrible! At first I was too pleased to see them—it was such a lonesome country! They were off a distance and I waved and shouted and tried to attract their attention. I thought surely they were two riders from a ranch somewhere around, and that I was real lucky to find help so soon. They stopped and I rode up to them. It never occurred to me who they might be!'

'How much did you tell them?'

'Too much,' she confessed sadly. 'I didn't like their looks, but I was so excited and so thankful to find someone that I just blurted out everything. I told them I had just gotten away from the Tobin bandits at Ghost Ridge and was trying to get to Crosscut to tell the law, that the bandits had you and Sam Beasley and that they had tried to rob the train and had killed Alcutt—'

'Let me hear that straight—you told Claude that I was sending you to Crosscut to get the law?'

'Yes. I guess that's the way I said it.' She stared up anxiously. 'That makes it worse for us, doesn't it?'

He was thinking that this was something Claude had not referred to yet, but Claude was not being fooled. Claude would play it watchful and do his own private figuring out. 'How did they break it to you, after you'd told them all that?'

Billie's eyes blazed. 'Mev Trout just laughed. Claude didn't laugh, though, he looked mad and said that I was about as close to Crosscut as I would get. Then they told me who they were.'

He saw Claude looking back for him from the corral. He lowered his voice and asked hurriedly, 'You still have Beasley's gun?'

'Yes, they didn't search me or anything— they just made me turn around and ride back here with them.'

'Hang on to that gun. When we start out, ride in the wagon and don't make any fuss.'

In another hour, when the sun was dipping bottom and laying broad shadows across the side of Ghost Ridge's rocky bones, the procession filed into the mesquites. The clearing and Alcutt's 'dobe house and wind-crippled pin oak sapling dropped back, then vanished from sight. Then the last of it, the high-shrieking windmill wheel, crazily racing to pull water for stock and humans no longer there, vanished, too. The wagons wound deeper into the lacy greenery of God's sorriest trees where Lincoln continued to hear the windmill screeching its mocking laughter in his ears, the dying echo of Ghost Ridge enjoying its private madness. It had brought the Tobins together again, he thought, and again sent them on their way. All but the dead, which it retained by custom, like the house's percentage of a game. Claude led the way—Claude with two Colts on his legs and a saddle-booted carbine and his restless hate for the world. Henny made a thin, weaving shadow on the high seat of the lead wagon, with Mev Trout out of sight under the canvas with a rifle in his lap. Uncle Dock handled the reins of the second wagon, with Billie huddled away from him at the far side of the blanket-padded seat. Lincoln and Ponch trailed the wagons. When they lurched across the rails and ties of the Fort Worth & Chihuahua in the first purple gloom of the big descending night, it seemed to Lincoln to have been years ago when he stepped down from the day coach along here. Away back in the dim past, when he was a man on a pleasant train trip, with a family at home and a respectable mission to do. Now the rails in the dark led nowhere. The destination tonight ran crossway with the tracks and his life and his mission. When the Tobin caravan bored into the dark mesquites again, southbound, he shifted in the saddle for a backward look but the night had already soaked up the railroad.

*　　　*　　　*

Ray Duncan of the Texas Rangers, newly assigned to the San Angelo district, sat at his desk in a makeshift office adjoining the jail and pored over an accumulation of telegraph reports from Fort Worth headquarters and from Marshal Kincaid out of Crosscut. The youthful Duncan, who was known to be as methodical in the paper study of a hard case as he was in meeting the more dangerous demands of his job, had doodled out a rough map while Eli McQuirter had rambled in talk. Duncan's pencil sketch included a dot labeled: *Crosscut*, railroad tracks east to Fort Worth, and another pencil dot marked: *GhostRidge*. Across the middle was a line for the Butterfield Trail, and a wavering pencil line ran toward the bottom of the sheet, ending in a question mark. Below that he had scrawled: *Laredo Area*.

McQuirter, special agent for the Fort Worth & Chihuahua, had already run dry of information on the attempted holdup at the East Fork wood stop. At the moment, the stocky young Ranger seemed more interested in McQuirter's remark that years ago a band of robbers had hidden out at Ghost Ridge near the wood stop. Rumors had claimed them to be the notorious Tobin gang. Duncan put down his pencil and shuffled through the sheaf of papers.

'This is one that interests me, Eli. Kincaid says they've identified one of the train passengers as Link Jones. At least, his description tallied with the kid bandit who rode with the Tobin crowd about ten years ago.'

The older man showed the effort of his mind groping back at the past. McQuirter allowed, then, that years ago the kid bandit's description had been well advertised and that Kincaid might be right.

'Say the man who got on the train at Crosscut was Link Jones,' Duncan speculated. 'He disappeared from the train at the wood stop. That gives us a Tobin earmark for the job. Not much, but a little. But to make it a shade stouter we have the Ghost Ridge place not far from the wood stop and we know the Tobin bunch used it for a hole-up at least once, a long time ago. We want the Tobins—bad. The ringleaders of that bunch have been our prime concern for a long time. The trail always peters out at the Rio Grande.'

'I don't envy you tryin' to head 'em off—if that's what you aim to tackle.'

Duncan looked at his map again. 'I might as well make out that these were the Tobins. A long shot, but we haven't got anything better.' He grinned briefly. 'Sometimes I play it by whim and it turns out about as well as by brains. Anyhow, it's the best we've got to work on.'

'You haven't got it narrowed down much, at that.'

Duncan tapped a finger on the question mark in his sketch. 'I know. Needle in a haystack out there.'

'Then I see you watching around Laredo,' McQuirter said shrewdly.

'It may be a waste of time, but I can afford a lot of time, if there's a chance in a thousand of getting between the Tobins and the river.'

'Let them come to you, huh?'

'I'd rather patrol the bottom end of a funnel than the top part.'

McQuirter said, 'I hear Mev Trout is out of the pen now. He was the only Tobin ever caught alive.'

Duncan glanced at the stack of telegraph reports. 'He headed west from Huntsville.'

'The fellow Beasley,' McQuirter mentioned, 'and the girl singer from Crosscut—reckon it's a sure thing they were in cahoots with the bunch?'

Duncan said something noncommittal, and McQuirter made his departure, telling the Ranger that he didn't envy him the hard riding in the wilds.

There were some things a Ranger kept to himself, even from a good friend—the little extra reserves of caution that seemed to count for something in the way the Rangers solved their cases and lived longer. Planting the man in prison for a while with Mev Trout, a few weeks before Trout's sentence ended, had not produced much, but Captain Rains at headquarters carried the permanent assignment on the Tobins and he was playing all possibilities. Duncan had studied the reports on that. The plant had come out with a few scraps of interest. One was that old Dock Tobin still lived, so far as Trout knew. Another seemed to nullify all the tall stories that had grown over the region about the kid killer with the band. For the way Trout had told it, Link Jones was no more than a scared-green boy who was forced to ride with the bunch, never pulled a trigger on a man all that time, and ran off from his unsavory relatives at the first chance he had and was never heard of again. Duncan scanned another report from Captain Rains, one that he had thought prudent not to mention to the railroad's special agent. *Railroad crew won't admit it*, Rains had telegraphed, *but some passengers claim train ran off and left three people at wood stop.* Duncan shifted uncomfortably every time he considered that. He would not have told a living human—in fact, he hardly admitted it to the inner Ray Duncan, Texas Ranger—that ever since his last trip to Crosscut the name and voice of Billie Ellis had stayed with him. Nobody would ever know that he had gone to the Longhorn three straight nights expressly to see her and had been smitten to the verge of asking for an introduction when he'd been forced to quickly leave town on urgent duty. Now they had her and a small-fry gambler named Beasley and a man they thought was Link Jones, all tied up neatly with the East Fork bandits. For a man who had kept trying to make up excuses for weeks to return to Crosscut and meet in person the vision he carried around in his memory, this turn of events at East Fork cooked him up one hell of a fine kettle of son of a gun.

When he rode southeast toward Laredo later that day, Ranger Duncan put it all out of his mind, except the hard thinking of how *he* would try to get to the border if he was an outlaw bunch with a price on his head. Playing it from the hunted men's shoes was a mental game he liked, and it often paid off. While he rode and mused on that, he absently hummed in rhythm to his horse's trotting hoofs a tuneful music-hall ditty that kept coming to mind, about a cowboy and a girl and a brindle bull.

CHAPTER THIRTEEN

Dock Tobin's word was the law of the clan, and the new law was that this returned nephew had equal status with Claude in running the outfit and planning the Byrd's Store raid.

In the grotesque workings of the old man's mind, a smart and able kinsman had returned to the fold. The grandeur of his clouded imagination saw his Nuevo Laredo bandit kingdom built prosperous and powerful again from its crumbling state of recent years.

Claude and Link would take hold. It would be like old times, not the way it had been of late with riffraff help, the good men vanishing, complaints that the law was closing in and the easy days of Texas raids a thing of the past. His mind clung to the old times; Tobin guns would recreate the old days. The big hacienda in the Madres would again wallow in pleasure and plenty.

The others listened, willing but dubious. They muttered that Texas was changing. Texas was whipping out the Indians and spreading west, and the good wild days when you could take over a town and loot it down to its last dollar—and good-looking women—seemed slipping away. Every foray across the Rio Grande in recent years had been more dangerous to accomplish, and smaller in loot.

Dock swept all that away with talk of big plans, accompanied by pulls on his whisky bottles, shared with the rest.

They had Claude, and Link was back and so was Mev Trout, and they would clean out Byrd's Store. That would be only the start. Just one damn Ranger in this whole Laredo country, they had learned. If they ran into that gent they'd take his ears back to dry in the sun on a string of *ancho* chili peppers.

But the big thing was, Link had come back. The boy had hurt his old uncle, running out on him that time. Blood kin ought to stick together. He'd rather have put a bullet through the boy's head, or had Claude or Mev do it, than have him run away. Dock had stayed drunk for a month and horsewhipped two peon ranch hands as outlet for his grief, so Ponch revealed, when young Link left.

But it was all fine now. Link had turned into a man to have around, a real Tobin leader. Experience behind him. He hadn't talked much about what he'd done, but they could guess it had been big deals. A hard one; smart, too—look at the way he'd found them at Ghost Ridge. Look at the shapely filly he'd latched on to for the good times ahead in the Madres.

Dock talked and dreamed, and the dissension, distrust, and suspicions of the others lapped up around him like little tongues of flames that he could not see.

There was only another day to go before

time to scout Byrd's place on the Butterfield Trail before the raid.

There had to be a showdown on that. Lincoln picked this morning to force it.

He stood spread-legged and tall, squared off against Claude, lean, unshaven, dirty, hard-jawed in the face and long in the gun arm hanging ready to the worn Colt on his leg—the gun that had killed Coaley Scull with three slugs in a dollar-size space in a target hidden by a wagon sheet.

'I'll make the advance scout on Byrd's,' he announced.

Claude backed down to nobody. To Uncle Dock, maybe. But not to his long-gone cousin whom he had plainly distrusted since the journey started.

'You'll stay in camp!' Claude retorted. 'I'm sending Trout in ahead to look the place over.'

'Don't be a damn fool. Everybody in the country has seen Trout.'

Trout squatted across the breakfast fire, listening but having eyes for nothing but Billie Ellis who sat apart from the men with her breakfast plate in her lap. She still wore Beasley's clothes but managed to look feminine in them, with her hair nicely combed, her lips tinted, and her cheeks powdered.

'They might spot me in there,' Trout agreed. 'Half of Texas came to the trial.'

Claude shot a distasteful glance to Ponch, and then to Henny. His expression showed the

189

immediate dismissal of them as incapable of making the important reconnoiter.

'You're not ridin' off anywhere,' he said thickly. 'I'll go, myself.'

Lincoln made a twisted smile at his cousin. 'You might have walked the streets of Crosscut and got away with it—but Old Man Byrd has seen you before, and you know it.'

Dock thundered, 'Link's right! He's the one to look over the place.'

Claude whirled on Dock, opened his mouth, thought better of what he meant to say. Angrily, he jerked up the blackened coffeepot from the coals and sloshed a steaming torrent into his tin cup.

The seven of them raggedly ringed the breakfast fire in the misty morning of their sixth day south of Ghost Ridge. Red trail dust layered their clothes and tinted the men's beards. Nights of riding and the short snatches of daytime sleeping had deepened the lines of their strained faces. Dock Tobin stalked over the gravel like an aged panther in a cage, forking food to his mouth. Ponch and Henny straggled off to spread their bedrolls. Trout's washed-out stare held on Billie like an invisible lariat stretched across to her, and Lincoln saw that she ate with the uncomfortable knowledge of Trout's continuous slack-jawed speculation, the goading hunger of a man not long out of a prison cell. Claude's restless black eyes worked everywhere, with never any pleasure in them for what he saw or for the thoughts behind them.

As Lincoln saw it, Byrd's Store was his big chance. After Byrd's there might never be sight of settlement, or even a human, between the Butterfield and the border, depending on the route Claude set. If he did not go in alone, to scout Byrd's before the raid, he would never have a chance again to set the trap. And it was imperative, too, as he saw it, to plant a warning of some kind with the people at Byrd's. He knew, almost as if the thought were printed on Claude's hard-boned face, that his cousin's mind crawled with suspicions; that in spite of Dock, he considered Lincoln and Billie as captives rather than confederates, at least until after they were across the Rio Grande. Claude had the animal instinct for caution of a prairie wolf many times chased and shot at, and some of Dock's old trait of almost being able to read a man's intentions through the bone of his skull.

Lincoln was reconciled to the loss of his money, and the trouble that would make for him and Lucy, at Odessa, probably the rest of their lives. Coaley, he speculated, had hidden the money somewhere in the brush around Ghost Ridge. And it's location died forever when Coaley died. But now his life—and Billie's—depended on what he could do between here and the border. It meant that he had to somehow wipe out the Tobins, and free themselves, and risk a try at clearing his name with the law.

With Claude's eyes on him day and night, and maybe with Trout assigned to watch him, too, the combinations of his problems seemed almost insurmountable in this hazy dawn.

Claude made a nervous thumb-jerk toward Billie. 'Tomorrow night she's goin' to be tied up in a wagon. We'll be close to the settlement.'

Lincoln whirled on him. 'Why do you say that?'

'She ran off from you once and headed for the law. She could try it again. I don't trust her.'

Billie laughed gaily, as if Claude was trying to be funny. 'I told you that I was just mad at Link. We patched it up, all sweet. Now quit worrying so much, Claude. I wouldn't leave Link again for anything.'

Claude looked unimpressed. Lincoln had played his role the best he knew how. So had Billie. But Claude's suspicions stayed broken out like a nettle rash.

Lincoln grinned sourly at his cousin. 'Don't be a damn fool, Claude. It's worth more to us to get over the border than anything else. I'm the one in this outfit they're lookin' for.'

Mev Trout said, 'Suppose we let him pull out and I'll take over his baggage.' His mouth formed a drooping smile for Billie.

She said sharply, 'I might have something to say about that.'

Lincoln looked down at Trout contemptuously. 'Coaley Scull had an idea something like yours. Any time you want to join Coaley in hell, try meddling with a Tobin's baggage.'

Uncle Dock and Claude would line up with him on that, at least if the woman issue hung between him and Trout. The pale killer's blinking eyes showed that he knew this, yet the challenge flung at him in front of Billie goaded him to his feet. Lincoln shifted sideways to Trout, watching his hands. Trout could use them both, left or right, fast as a rattler's strike.

'This is open range, Jones. I don't see no signs of your claim stakes. You ain't beddin' double.' Trout licked his dirt-crusted lips. His right elbow hooked out a little.

'The range is closed, as of now. You can get hurt, misreadin' the signs.'

Billie would have to be left alone in camp, when he rode to Byrd's. The issue with Trout had to be settled now, in advance of that.

Claude growled. 'Go cool off your craw, Mev.'

Lincoln drilled his gaze into Trout. 'Keep it cooled off, permanently. That's all the warning you're going to get.'

Dock bellowed, 'Get on up there on lookout, Trout! It's daylight and not a damn soul watchin' the country!'

Trout relaxed, shrugged, tried for a last word. 'Looked like open range to me,' he said

193

in forced good humor. 'You ain't bunked in the back of the wagon yet!'

Claude impatiently kicked dirt over the coals. 'Go stand your watch on the rim. And keep your damn eyes open, like I told you!' It seemed to Lincoln that a significant flicker of a glance went from Claude to Trout. The two of them walked away.

Five nights and a hundred miles lay behind the Tobins. Back there, too, dimming like the wagon tracks, lay the old lives of Lincoln Jones and Billie Ellis.

Link and his woman.

That was how the others looked on them. Her physical nearness each day, the circumstances that had brought them close together in their common dangers, had become a part of his other involvements. There was no other world existing outside their own small turbulent world of night travel, day hole-ups, and Tobins.

Dock hung back when Claude and Trout left and nagged Lincoln because Billie occupied her blankets alone in the back of the wagon. The old man took a gurgling draw in his ever-ready whisky bottle. 'By God, if you don't want her, I'll take her off your hands.' He stalked off to his bedroll behind a cedar clump.

Her protection hung by the strained thread of the guise that she was his woman. Lincoln saw the coloring come to Billie's cheeks from Dock's rough talk.

194

She murmured, 'If it would help matters any, for heaven's sake, *sleep* back there!'

He turned to her and his eyes burned hot, making her cheeks go pink again, but she said defiantly, 'If it keeps Trout away, what's the difference?'

He smiled one-sidedly. 'It would be crowded in there. You're a pretty woman, Billie.'

Their eyes held for a long moment. She reached a hand to his shoulder and pulled him down and kissed him full on the mouth.

She stepped away, just as quickly, and stood looking down at the campfire ashes. Then she turned and walked slowly to the wagon.

The mesquites had thinned a little, coming onto the Paint Rock roughs, making for better time. But smoldering animosity and general distrust dogged the creaking wagon wheels of the night travelers, until all were showing the strain. In the monotonous hours of riding, resentment had eaten at Claude and Dock over the train holdup failure. There was the galling prospect of having to retreat across the border empty-handed. Unless they did well at Byrd's.

The procession had crawled south by night, winding its ghostly course like a lost reptile through the eternal mesquites, the dry cuts, and sandstone ridges, across the Middle Concho which had trickle enough barely to water the horses, ever deeper into the empty, unwanted land, and now at dawn on this sixth day it curled up in the shallow pocket of an arroyo. Like in the other daytime hole-up camps, the wagons in the cut were out of sight of the country beyond the shielding cedars and mesquites on the rocky rim.

The sun was up now, making myriad shadows in the rocky arroyo. The others had rolled into their bedding, all except Trout who was standing early lookout on the brushy ledge over head. But Lincoln was not ready for sleep, and wandered down the cut toward the grassy patch where the hobbled *remuda* grazed.

When he walked out of the cedars again, and into the morning sun, he noticed that this far south of the railroad the air already had a warmer feel to it, heralding the coming summer. A buzzard floated high in its warm currents, a lazy black fly on the blue-cloud ceiling, and an early-working chaparral hen took out in a crazy run in pursuit of a frantic green lizard. He saw this, and more. Splotches of color ahead in a flat stretch of the ravine. Now he had his first glimpse of new blue-bonnets blooming, and a few red clusters among them of the early Indian paintbrush petals. He stared a long moment at this small sprinkling of wild flowers coming out of the arid earth, remembering.

Glancing up, he noticed a dark movement in the trees above the ravine. Mev Trout again. Trout had meandered down that way on his watch. Lincoln turned back, toward camp. The movement overhead drifted that way, too.

Back past the campfire ashes. Past the cedar clumps where the others slept. On to the last wagon, a distance off to itself. He swung over the tailgate, through the back opening of the wagon cover.

The last thing he saw, as he crawled in, was Mev Trout's shadowy outline, again hovering along the cedar-studded rim of the cut.

It was dark inside, and crowded with the cargo. Billie roused from the blankets on the floor between the feed sacks.

There was nowhere to fit his long frame except in the thin gap of space alongside Billie's pallet. She raised herself on her elbow. Her features took shape, her questioning eyes and her parted lips and her flesh where Sam Beasley's shirt gaped open. Even in the gloom, her eyes showed the color of the new bluebonnets he had seen, and her lips were as soft and red as the Indian paintbrush. She squirmed back slightly, the movement outlining her body under the blanket.

He did not have to speak much above a whisper, for her face was no more than two feet away.

'Were you asleep?'

'No. I—It's like that night in the shed.'

'That was a long time ago.'

'Ages. And poor Sam Beasley there—'

'Yeah. I guess he always thought—'

'I guess he did.'

'Anyhow, it got rid of Dock.'

197

Billie asked hesitantly, 'Did you decide to—make him think—'

'Not that, exactly.'

'You can sleep here, if that's space enough.'

Her face was very near. He touched her cheek with his fingers, lightly, and remembered the press of her kiss on his mouth.

In a moment she whispered, 'In here—with all that's happened, it's like we're shut off from the rest of the world, isn't it?'

He knew a desire to kiss her, and that the kiss would be returned, but he settled back to his space, for what he must say to her was difficult.

'I saw some wild flowers, down below. Bluebonnets and paintbrush. First I've seen.'

'That's nice—' She waited, then murmured amusedly, 'Did you come just to tell me that?'

'In a way,' he replied. 'They reminded me of something.'

'What did they remind you of, Lincoln?'

He listened intently for the sounds of anyone who might come lurking outside.

'Home, I guess. Odessa.'

Her voice sounded far away. 'Home—and your wife?'

'We always watch for the first one, about this time of year. They're right pretty, when they begin to break out all over the prairie. Last spring, Lucy and I saw the first bluebonnets on a flat over at a place we call Hatchet Mound. Same time we sighted them, I spotted an Indian standing in the rocks on top of that mound.'

198

'That's what these reminded you of, you mean?'

'I thought of the Indian watching us that time, yes. Same kind of flowers, while ago. Different Indian.'

'What?'

'Mev Trout. He was watching me.'

She stirred uneasily. 'Trout is watching you?'

'He's been tagging me. I just caught on for sure, while ago.'

'Why would that be?'

'It's just a guess, but I'd say Claude wants me watched. He wouldn't hesitate to kill me if he thought I was out to double-cross them. That's why I came to tell you. If anything happens to me, you're in a bad fix. You know that.' He felt her body stiffen in apprehension. He whispered, 'What I wanted to tell you now while I've got the chance—it would probably happen when we hit Byrd's Store, if they mean to try to get rid of me. If that happened, you try to get away from Dock's wagon at night. Run for the brush. Run anywhere, hide the best you can. They wouldn't spend too much time hunting you. Not after the store holdup. You've still got Beasley's gun. The Butterfield Trail is not far south of here. You try to do that, if I don't get back from scouting Byrd's.'

She started to speak but he touched her lips and the sound of the boot crunching gravel came to their ears. A low voice called, *'Hey, in the wagon! Link!'*

Lincoln saw the brim of a hat, then the head, materialize at the opening, and Trout looking for him in the shadows. Lincoln squirmed toward the opening, keeping his fisted six-gun out of sight under his thigh. 'What do you want, Trout?'

'Want to talk to you. Haven't got much time.'

'You picked a hell of a place.'

'Didn't want them to hear this.' Trout hesitated. 'What about the woman?'

'I trust her—guess you can, too.'

Trout said, 'No hard feelings, about a while ago?'

'That's up to you.'

The pale killer made his voice so low as to be almost inaudible. 'You know anybody that's lost a money belt full of currency?' Trout ended the question with a hollow laugh.

'Keep talking.' Trout was a strange one. Prison had not helped him any, either.

'How'd you like to know where to find it?'

'You damn well know the answer to that.'

'What would it be worth to you if it showed up in your bedroll?'

He tried to hear what lay behind Trout's words. Cautiously, he told Trout that he didn't have much to offer. What did he have in mind as a price?

Trout's deep-set blank stare slid off Lincoln, and onto Billie's blanketed shape. 'You got

200

plenty to offer, if you want your money very bad.'

He heard Billie's breath flow out. Anger burned Lincoln's stomach like a raw drink as Trout's meaning hit. Trout said softly, 'Six hundred dollars. You're not likely to get it back unless it's me that swings it.'

It was a lot of money, all right. More than Trout knew. He felt Billie's eyes on him.

Lincoln said, 'You mean what I think you mean?'

Trout growled thickly, 'Five years in prison is a long time.'

With strained control of his voice, Lincoln said, 'You considered there might be another party with a say-so in this?'

'She's your woman!' Trout gritted. 'What the hell—That money important to you or ain't it?'

So that made two of them, now. Dock and Trout. The slinking, pale-eyed man at the foot of the wagon, with his jaw hanging slack from a hunger that prodded him to any extreme. His next offer, if this was refused, would likely as not be a bullet in the back, and taking his chances on winding up with the prize.

'It'll take some talking over,' Lincoln said carefully. 'I'll let you know.'

'Don't wait too long. I know where the money is now, but it's not nailed down.'

The pale features faded from sight and they could hear Trout moving through the brush as he worked his way back up to the rim. Lincoln turned back to Billie, showing a tight grin, which infuriated her. She demanded indignantly, 'Was that jailbird trying to *buy* me?'

He could understand her indignation but she had missed the big point. Trout had settled one worry, at least.

The money was somewhere around, in the wagons, or being carried by Ponch or Henny. Not hidden in the brush at the Ghost Ridge place by Coaley, which possibility had gnawed at him every mile of the travel southward. Coaley had not taken the money after all—and the other two who might have had the same chance to rob the valise that night were Ponch and Henny. Trout evidently had spotted the money belt on one of them, or in their gear, and the idea of a trade with Lincoln was born in his one-track mind.

Billie was still quivering with anger at Trout's cold-blooded audacity, doubly infuriating because it had taken place within her own sight and hearing.

'He's crazy! Does he think that's all he has to do?'

'Down in the Madres, at Dock's place, they don't think much about buying and selling the Mexican girls. The way Trout sees it, he made a fair offer to me to turn you over to him.'

Her tensely murmured question was inevitable. 'Are you?'

The Odessa frontier, his neighbors and Lucy and home were foggy wisps of unrealities in another world, beyond a border he could not easily cross again. Without the money he could not return, but neither could he return it ransomed in a ruthless Tobin way. The money was only a part of it, now. The road back across the border to his Odessa life could never be traveled until his name was cleared and the Tobins dead or in the hands of the law. He answered Billie. 'That's a foolish question.'

She whispered, 'I'm grateful to you. For that.' He caught the faint irony when she added slowly, 'That's the same money I was about halfway willing to help Sam steal. I guess it was me, and not Mev Trout, that wrote my own price tag.' She sighed. 'A lesson somewhere in that. Not that I needed another one, after all that's happened!'

'Not the only six-hundred-dollar mistake ever made in Texas,' he replied quietly. 'I know somebody who thought it represented how a man was all square with the world and could go anywhere and face anybody—'

Suddenly, she seized blindly at his shoulders, leaning across to him and burying her face in his chest. 'Don't go into Byrd's alone, Lincoln! Something could happen to you—you might never come back!'

Gently, he lifted her aside and edged toward the opening at the end of the wagon. 'I expect to make it all right. But just in case I don't, and you have trouble—push that little gun of Beasley's right close up to Dock's stomach, or Trout's, whichever one you have to deal with, and pull the trigger slow, so you won't miss.'

CHAPTER FOURTEEN

The night they swung southwest to come out of the roughs below Byrd's Store was a warm and starry one. The milky light leavened the harshness of the wastes, touching the rocky spines of the ridges, the greasewood and the giant prickly-pear clumps, with guileless coatings of limpid tranquillity. In the velvet silence of the Indian dawn the land for a little while lost its malignity. The daytime scars were covered up, and the rattlers, coyotes, tarantulas, buzzards, and gaunt, starved jack rabbits were burrowed unseen into the crust of the night. Only the Tobin outlaws were on the move to disturb the vast stillness, the illusion of peace that sheeted the lonely world between the Butterfield Trail and the Mexican Border.

Then this alien crawler of mounted shadows, swaying canvas-topped wagons, and sleepy-footed horses, burrowed in, too, and bunched upon itself in a familiar nocturnal submerging against the eyes of the coming day. Only this day would be different.

This day, thought Lincoln, would have ten

delayed years packed into it before the sun went down. Every animal had to crawl into its last hole-up before dying. *Make it a good one, Dock; dig in good and deep, Claude.* And as he silently consigned his hated kin to his hoped-for end of their journey, the camp was doing just that, digging in, and he was helping.

By sunup, the wagons were hidden in a brush-choked ravine, the horses and teams picketed in shielding cedar breaks, and the breakfast fire quickly used for its purpose and extinguished. Ponch rode in from his far-back watch after the Butterfield crossing, to report that there had been no sign of living thing in the night after the wagons had hurried across the open spaces flanking the Butterfield tracks.

So they felt sure that the swing around south of Byrd's had been made unseen, that the stage-line settlement just four miles north slept serenely, unaware that the Tobins roosted within quick striking distance.

Lincoln had gained his point, that he would be the one to make the casing trip into Byrd's. The logic of his argument appeared to stand up, despite Claude's surly dissatisfaction. Claude himself might be recognizable to a few people down there. Mev Trout had the unmistakable looks of a bad man, a hired two-gun killer, written all over him and could never change that look. Ponch and Henny had the stamp, too, that would never pass for a transient ranch hand innocently passing

205

through the country westbound from San Antonio. Lincoln was the man to go. Yet the obstinate uneasiness showed in all of them, especially in Claude, that there was somehow danger in giving the alien Odessa man this freedom.

He had no opportunity to speak again with Billie alone. What final things were said had to be done with meaningful eye work, for the others ringed them with the tawny yellow looks of a watchful wolf pack, showing half confidence, half claws, for one of their off-color breed.

Dock was drunk, with his mind turning mean, the floodgates of old suspicions and resentments swinging open. This was the stage of drunkenness the old man invariably attained, as they all knew, when there was a doubted confederate to kill, a greaser ranch slave to be whipped, or a lustful orgy to be put on in the locked inner rooms of the Madre house whose cold 'dobe walls had looked down on so much in the Tobins' good years. With the whisky firing his mind and muscle, Dock swelled bigger in size. His massive head, bushy gray in matted whiskers long unshaven, gave him the appearance of a giant animal that had risen to its hind feet. He stalked upon Lincoln.

'Why did you come back, boy?'

At first, the accusing question confused Lincoln, who was thinking only of the time at hand.

'Why did you come to Ghost Ridge? You run away, that time. I'd 'a rather killed you, boy, than have you done that. What you back here for, Link?' An ancient suspicion, or a deep-rooted knowing that the young boy had never been *with* him in heart, came out of tangled cover. The reddish pupils in nests of wild gray brows burned malevolently into him. Burning deep to find the truth.

Dock breathed wetly, his red mouth agape in the whiskered matting. *'What you aimin' to do to us when you get to Byrd's?'*

No other man present, the ones watching, could have done it. But they saw their Odessa kinsman do it, although to Lincoln it was nothing more than a mechanical release of reckless anger, a plain being fed up with Dock, with the badgering, with the whole strain of coping with fangs bared at him from all sides. He smashed his open hand solidly into Dock's chest and shoved the old man away.

'What d'you mean—what am I going to do at Byrd's?' He snarled out the words at Dock, around the others. 'That's been settled, and now I'm going in, and I'm tired of your badgerin'.' He saw Dock's old frame sag in front of him. The red coals turned blank, the buffalo-big head swung slowly from side to side.

'Don't get sore, boy. You go scout Byrd's— You're the one to do it, Link.'

The others stared in disbelief at the miracle

of Lincoln still alive.

Claude said through set teeth, 'You better be damn sure you do it right.'

Lincoln whirled on Claude. 'You think anybody here can tell me better what to do in there?'

Claude's jaw knots formed hard lumps of belligerence. 'I want this job cased right, by God—'

Dock had turned his attention to working the whisky bottle out of the side pocket of his coat. Intent on this, he rumbled without turning, 'Don't let 'em take you, Link—You watch Cal Byrd. He's mean.'

'Don't forget to come back, either.' Claude spat to one side, not changing his eye hold. 'This thing'd better go off right.'

Lincoln met his hard glare for a moment, then moved impatiently. 'To hell with this! What's the matter with you two-bit border jumpers—your guts unravelin' out on you when there's a big one to pull? I'm the one's going in there where somebody might want to wrap a noose around my neck.' He threw a contemptuous jerk of his thumb over his shoulder at their leader. 'Let the old bastard embalm himself and you tighten up this outfit, Claude. Otherwise we'll all be draggin' back across the Rio like a sick bunch of mudcats without a damn dollar to show for the trip. Now I've heard all the damn calf-bleatin' I want to hear!'

He turned his back on the lot, gave a vicious tightening jerk to the cinch strap of his fresh mustang, and in one motion stirruped his boot, legged into the saddle, and brought the bobbling head of the animal around in rein control. On the horse, his land-bound height and awkwardness seemed to drain off him. Now he was a blend of man, saddle, and horseflesh, a unit with the hide and muscles under him, feeling the way he liked to feel, up where a man belonged. He knew with the salty taste in his mouth of unleashed challenge to them that none was going to contest his going. He tossed one quick look to Billie, now sunk in a fragile white-faced huddle on a wagon tongue, without risking a softening in his eyes that he momentarily felt in his chest. Then that, too, was gone.

Claude started to say, 'Main thing, find out if—'

'I know,' he interrupted. 'If they got money on hand, where Byrd and his family sleep, how many horses there, how many people, and how many guns they could count on.' He looked them over, his distaste showing. 'Try to be ready when I get back—We want no hammerheaded fools dropping their bridles on this, like at East Fork.' He shot that at Ponch and Henny. And saw that it hurt. Dock pointed his head up, waving it against the light, and said that Link was mighty right.

Trout wasn't around. Lincoln demanded,

'Where the hell's Mev?'

Claude answered with a gesture toward the cedars. 'Seein' about the horses.'

'I'll hold you responsible, Claude—keep him away from her.'

He leaned in the saddle to take the first dug-in jump of the mustang as he slammed the spurs home, and the thorn-scarred pony stretched its neck, put its belly to the weeds, and tore, scrambling upgrade, through the greasewood clumps, over the ridge, and into the sunlight of the mesquites in the upper flat.

He worked north through the mesquites, holding to a walk for there was no reason to hurry and the more run he saved in the horse, the better, in case it was needed later. He stretched the ride by a long circle east, so he could come into Byrd's from that direction. The last mile or so he rode the ribbons of tracks that marked the Butterfield route from San Antonio.

Byrd's proved to be nothing more than a couple of frame buildings, a sizable corral, and a few shacks. Their location was signaled by a scattering of cottonwoods and poplars around the water hole on Turkey Creek.

Riding in, watching everywhere from under his hatbrim, he saw the rambling paint-peeled structure that would be the store itself, the built-on living-quarters, the stage line's barn across the road and its horse pens of heavy timbers, a couple of box frame shacks on the creek crossing, and a trickle of smoke from a dilapidated open-front shed with the earmarks of a blacksmith shop.

The tie rail in front of the store was deserted of horses, and the whole place looked branded with futility as if Cal Byrd had made a mistake in locating in this God-forsaken bottom of Texas and all concerned had given up.

Outward looks could be deceptive, though. What this lost soul of a settlement might know about the outside world would depend on when the stage, or trade wagons, or a transient rider, had last come along—whether news had drifted this far off about the train bandits and the reappearance of Link Jones as a wanted man.

He tied reins at the rail, taking his time, trying to feel behind him toward the stage barn across the ruts with the back of his head, while his eyes worked the store front. He felt rather than saw movement over there, and turned. A man plodded through the dust inside the corral, working among a dozen milling horses. He waved a careless gesture across to Lincoln, and went on about his work.

The inside of the store was dim-lighted and odorous of cattle hides, coal oil, stale cheese, and a chorus of other strident smells. Lincoln moved away from the door light at his back, then paused to get his sight adjusted to the gloom. Even before he heard movements of someone far back in the building, he caught

211

sight of the squat iron safe against the wall of a railed-in office space. That would be the Butterfield 'bank,' he guessed, the place where money shipments were held between stage connections, the stopover depository for valuables, for the traders and travelers who did business between Sanantone and San Angelo, and gave Byrd's its main excuse for being.

A hell of a bank, he thought, and a hell of a chance of protection the place had. A guttural voice sounded behind him.

'Don't make any snap judgment, *amigo*.'

He shifted, not too fast, to see the speaker. Instead of the man he expected to go with that thick voice, he beheld a massive woman padding out of the shadowy opening of the lean-to room. Her fat arms nursed a sawed-off shotgun. The dark Mexican flesh billowed over her in ponderous rolls, bulging her draping calico that hung like an enormous sack from shoulders to shapeless ankles. Crow-black hair dangled untended to her shoulders. The sleepy black eye dots in the dark face held languid control of him as she lumbered around the counter.

Lincoln touched his hatbrim, still not too fast in the movement. She looked him over again, then released the shotgun to the counter top.

'Cal will be here in a minute.'

'No hurry, señora. I'm just resting, mostly. Just rode in.'

212

'No stage till Saturday.'

'When did the last one come through?'

'Day before yesterday. Santone one. Saturday be westbound day.'

Day before yesterday. Unlikely, that soon, to have word of the Link Jones hunt but possible. He took his hat off, wiped at the sweat of the inner band, and grinned crookedly at the watchful woman.

'You sort of gave me a spook, that sawed-off on me.'

As if she had counted the signs and found the weather clear, she settled her weight relaxedly against the counter. 'Stranger ridin' in, we always watch. What the windows are for. Cal or me, one. Habit out here.' She added tonelessy, 'Looked like you was tryin' to see a lot, ridin' in. Headed far?'

'San Angelo way.'

The movements from the back turned into thudding bootsteps. The man who approached through the clutter stretching back to the storage section was bound to be Cal Byrd himself. A square-built short man, hard black eyes, black mustaches drooping, high-waisted gun belt hanging his holstered gun nearly to the front of his stomach.

The woman said, 'He's ridin' through.'

Byrd nodded, neither friendly nor unfriendly. Lincoln motioned to the massive keg behind the counter. 'A schooner of that *cerveza* wouldn't taste bad.' The woman drew

213

the beer.

Byrd said, 'You come far?'

'Laredo. Understand there's no stage till Saturday.'

'They'll pen your horse.' Byrd motioned across the street. 'They can bunk you, too, if you want to stay over.'

He sipped on the tepid beer. 'Main thing, I got some money on me I wanted to send. You've got a safe place to keep it, I reckon, till the stage picks it up?'

Both sets of eyes drifted to the iron safe and back on Lincoln. *Money in there now.*

Byrd shuffled to the counter. At his mumbled words the woman turned and filled another schooner at the keg.

Byrd said, 'We can oblige you. How much and where to?'

Lincoln repeated, 'Good safe place to keep it?'

Byrd glanced again at the safe. 'Serves the Buttterfield Line, well enough. Reckon it will take care of yours.'

The shrill voices of children rose briefly, somewhere out at the back. Lincoln asked, '*Muchachos?*'

'*Tres.*'

Lincoln indicated himself. '*Dos.*' He gestured with his palm, waist-high.

The woman mumbled, 'I go to the kitchen, Papa. He will be hungry.'

An elderly Mexican came in at the front,

214

hung his straw sombrero on a nail, and went lazily to work at rolling up a stack of dried steer hides. Byrd's helper also wore a gun.

Lincoln took his chance now and dropped the casual question. 'You're a far distance from the law here. You ever worry about bandits holding you up for the money shipment?'

The store owner's shaggy brows plowed to a frown. 'Not especially. Why?'

He would give Byrd the whole story. The best way to clear Link Jones's name was to set a trap, with Byrd's help, that would catch the Tobin bunch. Then he would run his horse all the way back to the wagon camp to take charge of Dock before harm could come to Billie. If Byrd believed him, tonight he would lead them in ambush here.

The Mexican helper seemed staked to the counter where the sawed-off shotgun lay. It would be better if he could get Byrd alone.

'Mind going across with me, while I take my horse over to be fed? The money I wanted to leave with you is in my saddle roll.'

Byrd grunted and let Lincoln go ahead of him out the door. He could feel the caution in the store man, as Byrd trailed him down the steps. Lincoln led the horse across the road toward the barn. The door of the barn hung open. Fifty paces down the road an overalled man lounged in the opening of the blacksmith's shop. Half visible around the

215

corner of the barn, as they approached the pens, was a saddled mount, reined to a sapling, among the small growth there.

They had almost reached the corral gate when Lincoln saw the movement in the shadowed insides of the barn doorway. A waiting black figure lazily separated itself from the gloom and leaned against the doorframe.

As Lincoln looked up, pale, drawn lips released a thin stream of cigarette smoke. Mev Trout hitched his gun belt with its double holster weights.

'*Buenas tardes*, Byrd.' Trout's voice was a toneless drawl. 'Sell a man a little horse feed?'

They both slowed their stride. Lincoln felt the hackles crawl on his neck. Byrd squinted.

'It's Mev Trout—ain't it?'

'You got a good memory for faces.'

Byrd said unpleasantly, 'Saw you at the trial at Uvalde. When did you get out?'

Trout smiled mockingly. 'Just recent. Paid my debt, free man now, law-abidin' as hell.'

Questions reeled through Lincoln's mind. *Why did he come here? What did he want?*

Byrd nodded shortly. 'That's good. I'll sell you feed, Trout. Then I'd just as soon for you to ride on.'

The man in the doorway shrugged. 'Suits me. Just passin' through, anyhow.' Then, as if noticing Lincoln for the first time, Trout murmured, 'Who's your friend, Cal? Looks familiar.'

Byrd murmured something noncommittal and stalked across to the gate, which he opened, letting himself in, and trudged out of sight around the corner, calling loudly for Juan to come sell some horse feed.

CHAPTER FIFTEEN

Trout was not leaning against the doorframe now. He stood erect, balanced with his feet apart, his hands hanging beside the two gun butts and the smile gone off his face. Lincoln slowly switched the bridle reins to his left hand and repeated his first low-spoken question.

Trout retorted, 'You're a smart *hombre*—you ought to be able to guess.'

'Claude?'

'Yeah. He sent me to follow you.'

'All the way in to here?'

'Just to the edge of the brush back yonder. Coming on in was my idea.'

Lincoln's ears shrilled it at him, the truth taking shape.

'You didn't have the guts to try it back there, did you?'

Trout didn't care now. Everything was like Trout wanted it. 'Not with Dock and Claude around. This way I can't lose.'

Lincoln kept watching Trout's face, but seeing the gun hands. 'You'll still have 'em to

217

face.'

'What the hell if I do?' The thin lips tightened to a pleased smile. 'They done it here—' He tilted his head to indicate all of Byrd's. 'Not me. They spotted Link Jones and started shooting. I just heard it from out in the brush. Who's to tell it different?'

Lincoln slid a glance to the gate and back, hearing men talking in the pen, but Byrd was still out of sight.

'How you aim to try it?' But he already knew. Trout had figured it slick.

'It'll all at once dawn on me that you're the outlaw Link Jones everybody's huntin'. You can be captured or try to run—you name it.'

He measured the hang of Trout's hands, the steps it would take to duck to the side of his horse.

Trout murmured, 'Don't start nothin'.'

Lincoln said, 'You couldn't wait, could you? I might have taken you up on the money deal.'

'This is better. This way I'll get both.'

Boots thumped the ground at the corner. Cal Byrd came out. A stocky man followed him. This one asked, 'Which wanted to buy the feed?'

Trout said, 'Just been dawning on me, Byrd—You know who this gent is?'

He couldn't watch them all at once. His hands felt like tree stumps, his six-gun like it was twenty feet out of reach.

Byrd mumbled something. Trout gritted,

'*It's Link Jones—the bandit!*'

'Link Jones?'

'They're huntin' him all over Texas!'

Byrd said, 'Watch 'im, Juan!'

Juan, the stocky man, exclaimed, 'Damn if he ain't—the stage driver told me about him the other day! Fits the—'

'He's a killer!' Trout warned. 'Big reward!'

'Byrd, wait just a minute, now—'

Byrd had his Colt out. 'Get his gun off him, Juan—Careful!'

A voice bellowed from the store front: 'Dinner's ready for you, señor!'

Running feet, a noise enough for a cavalry charge, scurried past Cal Byrd's massive wife. Young voices whooped, and three overalled kids raced across the road, carrying on a mighty chatter and a rowdy shoving among themselves as they tore toward the group. The horse spooked and began plunging. Lincoln sorted the reins by the feel of his left fingers, and made hidden jerks on the left line. The mustang sawed, fighting the bridle. The three Byrd kids plowed to a dusty stop, their father yelling a warning.

The mustang, panicked by the commotion, fought the bridle tugs, crowding Lincoln back, circling. And as the horse plunged alongside he made his draw.

The shielding horse blocked Trout's sight of him for the second it took for his six-gun to come up, and by then anything that Trout

219

could do was a second too late. Lincoln triggered with the gun close under the mount's neck. Trout got half-out with his right-hand gun. He stretched up tall and bloated from the slug impact into his chest, and Lincoln fired again, blasting Trout in a dead man's fall in the barn opening. The mustang reared with the explosions and he fought to hold the reins, whirling with the horse, clambering to keep footing close against the animal, to keep the spooked horse between him and Byrd and Juan. The kids scattered, running between the house and Byrd.

Like storm sounds in his ears, he heard the tumult, the woman's bellowing voice to the children to get out of the way, the rattle of the mustang's hoofs. All the confusion happened in seconds—from the mustang's first scare to his shooting Trout to the final scramble around the barn corner, struggling to stay close to the offside of the bucking horse, never giving Byrd or Juan a target. Then he was clawing his way into the saddle, planting the spurs, and the mustang let his fright loose in the dead run for the saplings back of the barn. One gun blasted behind him. The slug moaned past his side, and then he was in the trees, and the other gunshots from the road only added oil to the mustang's running muscles.

He waited out the afternoon hidden in a gully far west of Byrd's, then rode circling through the mesquites, and reached camp just before sundown. Billie hurried to him, relief showing in her eyes. Some of her eager welcome, too, was strain from being alone with the Tobins through the day, and he pressured her arm reassuringly as she turned to walk beside him.

Claude wanted to know things, fast. He shot the questions and Lincoln answered. Lincoln told it as if he had made his appraisal of Byrd's exactly according to plan. A successful strike could be made that night, he said.

If Byrd was as smart as he figured him to be, the warning of a holdup try had been planted. Enough, he hoped, that Byrd would have his men posted tonight, just in case. The presence of Link Jones there, the killing of Trout, the question that had been asked about the money box—If Byrd had any gumption at all, he would be on the lookout. And he thought Byrd had gumption.

If he could keep himself from getting trapped or killed, if he could maneuver Claude and Ponch and Henny into an ambush, and get back to Dock and Billie, that would be the last of the Tobin outlaws.

They talked it over. Dock Tobin beamed, pleased with the prospects. Claude went over it again, digging.

'How come you stayed all day?'

'Took my time. Byrd's wife fixed a big dinner. Played with their three kids awhile. Took time to get the whole lay.'

After a time, the question came he had been expecting. Claude had been throwing anxious glances at the ravine edge.

'You see anything of Mev anywhere, on your way back?'

Lincoln looked surprised. 'No. Why? He missing?'

'Haven't seen him lately,' Claude admitted.

Lincoln demanded, 'You mean you let him ride out of here?'

'He thought he'd take a look around,' Claude evaded.

Dock stormed. 'That damn Trout! I don't like him going off that way, Claude. Where is he?'

Claude muttered, 'How in hell do I know?'

Lincoln confronted Claude with a show of anger. 'You didn't send Trout to trail me into Byrd's, did you?'

'Why, hell, no!' he blustered.

'He didn't have the guts to ride on this job tonight!' Dock decided. 'Damn jailbird turned yellow-livered.'

It was time to start preparations. Lincoln left Claude to his own worries on what might have happened to Trout. Supper was eaten hurriedly. The teams were hitched to the wagons so no time would be wasted on that when they got back from the holdup. Dock stalked about, hitting his bottle again in the high tension of the hour, telling them how to do it. Four fresh horses were brought out and saddled, and the others secured to the wagon tailgates by lead ropes.

Lincoln managed only a minute alone with Billie. 'If it goes right,' he whispered, 'I'll be back. The others won't. And that'll be the end of this.'

She caught his arms, turning her worried eyes up to him, and tried to make a smile that only turned into lip quivers.

'You got the little revolver?'

She nodded. 'In my pocket.'

'If you have to, use it.'

She held to him when he tried to turn. He saw the face strained up to him, and the plea in her eyes, and her reluctance for the start of what the night might bring. He stooped to the white face, and kissed her.

Claude called hoarsely, 'Come on—time to ride!'

*   *   *

At a back table in the Rio Saloon at Laredo, Ranger Ray Duncan made pencil lines on his map. Sheriff Joe Berra was saying, 'Wagons can't ford there, nor there, and not up here at Rocky Junction, either. Quicksand.' He punched at spots on the wavy line marked: *Rio Grande*. Then he mused, 'What the hell would they be doing in wagons, I wonder?'

Duncan said, 'Search me. Headquarters just wired somebody had found wagon tracks crossing the railroad, going on south to nowhere. I'm playing it that way, for lack of something better. Now here's the way I dope it, sheriff. If I'm in wagons and I got to funnel down to some place where I can get across the river, I'd take this route.' He indicated a line. 'By now, I'd maybe be somewhere around here.' He made a circle between Laredo and the Butterfield.

Berra said, 'I dug back in all the files we got. Funny thing, to me—how this Link Jones kid disappeared in thin air once. Never was heard of again. Not till the other day. You reckon he's been with the Tobins all this time?'

Ranger Duncan let a slight grin form on his boyish, weathered face. 'Damndest thing you ever heard of, sheriff. Let me show you something.' He pulled papers out of various pockets—telegrams from Fort Worth, letters, and finally a folded newspaper clipping. 'This came in the mail from headquarters today.'

He handed this across the table. 'We already knew that the Link Jones kid-outlaw business was a myth. But read this—it'll give you an idea of where he disappeared to and what became of him.'

Before Berra adjusted his steel-rimmed spectacles and started reading, he asked, 'What'd you make of it, Ray—about the girl singer and the fellow, Beasley, that vanished off the train?'

Duncan looked uncomfortable. 'That girl

was all right,' he muttered. 'She wasn't in with any outlaws.'

'You knew her, did you?'

Duncan felt foolish. No way to tell Berra how he had watched Billie Ellis through three nights of performances in Crosscut and had carried around thoughts of her ever since. He said, 'Oh, hell—read that stuff, sheriff. I got to be riding up the country.'

Berra read.

'I might as well mosey along with you,' he said gruffly. 'Feel like I ought to look out after any Ranger when he's in my country. Need to get out a little, anyhow.'

'Be glad to have your company. Need a good sheriff along, to keep me from getting lost. As a matter of fact,' Duncan grinned, 'I've already ordered two pack horses to be ready for us to strike out tonight. Let me pay for the beer.'

CHAPTER SIXTEEN

Lincoln said, 'Pull in this way, it'll bring us up alongside the barn, in the trees.'

'I want the horses right at the store,' Claude said. 'You and Ponch hit the back, Henny and me at the front.'

Ponch grumbled. 'Too damn much starlight.'

Henny made a nervous laugh. 'Who in hell

225

wants to die in the dark?'

Ponch called Henny a series of names in Spanish.

'Shut up!' Claude already had his gun out. The buildings took ghostly forms. Claude was to handle Byrd himself, when they got inside, overseeing the opening of the safe. The others were to stand lookout, front and back. Claude repeated, 'Kill any damn thing that moves sudden.'

Lincoln said, 'Give us about three minutes.' He and Ponch walked their horses through the trees, circling toward the rear of the store.

If you've set a trap, Byrd, for God's sake, get to springing it!

Back of the store, Ponch said, 'About here. Hitch to this post. Now, let's hit 'em!'

Lincoln followed Ponch, feeling that his shoulders made a bullet target as wide as Byrd's house. If Byrd was caught napping, and the holdup got started, he would have to turn to Claude and the others. With Byrd's help he might get top hand. The certain thing was, nobody was going to hurt Byrd, nor his wife, and none of those kids.

His straining ears caught a faint rustle of sound, somewhere in the shadowed corner.

Byrd was not caught napping. All at once the whole night unraveled in thunderous hostility. Three quick shots sounded at the front of the building. Ponch whirled and jumped a foot off the ground. Claude and Henny had met

226

trouble. Ponch and Lincoln turned back together, crouching. Running horses sounded somewhere.

Spinning toward the corner, Lincoln saw the figure in the shadows, and a rifle, raised. He dived sideways to the ground. The rifle licked out a fiery streak.

Ponch flattened against the wall. Guns roared again toward the road.

The back door opened.

Lincoln saw the massive figure outlined there. Ponch brought his six-gun around.

'No, Ponch! A woman—she's—'

The woman held a shotgun, a plain target in the doorway. Ponch's gun hand lifted.

Mrs Byrd's voice. A cautious call: 'Juan— You there?'

Ponch was going to kill her. Only he wasn't. Lincoln took snap aim from the hip, throwing the slug into Ponch at close quarters. He heard the *slap* sound of the bullet as it smacked Ponch to earth. The door slammed. The rifle cracked from the house corner, and something spun Lincoln sideways with a hard blow on his shoulder. He snapped a shot over the head of the shadow, to drive it to cover, and ran.

He stumbled, knees buckling, and tried to grab at the fire in his left shoulder. A rifle bullet dusted dirt in his eyes. He ran, momentarily lost, all turned around. Then a plunging horse was in his face. His horse.

He made a slow, tortuous search for the

227

reins. A long hunt for a stirrup to get his foot into. The night went black. Something sticky spread down his arm. He clung to the saddle, feeling the wind of running speed in his face. Tree shadows flashed past and their thorny branches lashed him.

He had to get to Billie. Had to handle Dock now. No way of knowing if Claude and Henny had escaped. The black world spun crazily. Hang on. *Hang on!* He tried to set a course through the spinning night.

A long time later he felt the horse bunch to its haunches, taking the downgrade of the ravine. Thin starlight bathed the wagons, horses, Uncle Dock's towering figure. Claude and Henny were there. Byrd had started the shooting too soon.

Claude snarled, 'Where's Ponch? They get him?'

Dock cursed. 'No guts. You all let 'em run you off.'

'They were set for us,' Henny whined.

It seemed like a mile from the saddle to the ground.

Henny said, 'Link's hit. I got grazed, too. Across my back.'

'Damn lucky we got out alive!' Claude made no move to help.

Lincoln tried to stand on his feet.

'Where's Billie?'

Claude demanded, 'You have anything to do with that reception we got?'

228

Dock lumbered up to show something in his hand. The .32 revolver. Lincoln saw through the fog in his eyes the movement at the wagon. Billie crawled over the seat and rushed to him.

The old man wagged the revolver. 'The damn little hellcat tried to shoot me!'

Billie buried her face against his chest. 'Lincoln—he—I had to try to use the gun—but he took it away before I could—'

He pushed her back to search her face, forcing his muscles to keep him on his feet.

'I fought him off!' she whispered. 'I kept fighting him—then Claude and Henny came—'

He murmured with a thick tongue, 'That's good, Billie.'

'*You're hurt!* You're bleeding!'

Dock bawled, 'Get the wagons moving!'

He made it to a wagon wheel, turned, and slumped against it.

Claude watched. 'Let him bleed to death. I think the sonofabitch set that trap for us!'

Billie tugged off his jacket, tore at his shirt, and he fought to keep his footing. She ripped off the sleeve. Her hands worked fast to plug a wad of cloth into the wound, and the blood trickle stopped. She tied the bandage.

'Dump him in the back!' Claude shoved Billie away. Claude and Henny dragged him up and over into the wagon.

Stretched in the wagon bed, he saw Henny climb to the wagon seat. The last he heard was

Dock's drunken voice, ordering Billie to Dock's wagon, then a string of endless profanity for the failure at Byrd's, for the hellcat who tried to shoot him, for Trout's disappearance, and for Ponch's letting himself get shot. The Tobin comeback had crumbled.

Something else came spinning in his head. As he succumbed to engulfing drowsiness, the knowledge flooded over the pain that he knew now where his money belt was. Then his world washed out in total blackness.

*   *   *

The wagon creaked and swayed. He floated out of the depths with a dull throbbing in his shoulder, with the roll of the wagon under him.

The battle at the store, the killing of Trout and of Ponch—these were fog wisps in his brain. He had no conception of how long the travel had been underway. But his last conscious thought came back vividly strong. *The money.*

Like a man possessed by a hallucination from high fever, he stared at Henny's back.

Henny. Something he had seen when Henny had settled to the seat and started up the team. Henny's back—the ripped place across his shirt where the bullet had sliced his clothes. The parted cloth. The projecting edge of the money belt. The telltale bulge. *Henny was the one!* Here was the crafty member who had succumbed to the temptation of robbing the valise in the Ghost Ridge shed. Henny taking the big risk, latching on to the six hundred dollars.

He stared at Henny's back, no more than six feet in front of him. The gap in Henny's shirt. Moonlight, now. Enough to play on Henny's ripped clothes, Henny's secret revealed.

He crawled forward. His money there made an obsession that pulled him along the wagon bed. Henny must have heard him above the wheel creakings.

He turned as Lincoln reached for him.

'Git back down!'

'The money, Henny!'

A gun somewhere. He should have pulled his own. The gun—

It was in Henny's fist.

'My money—'

'Claude said kill you if you made trouble!'

'The money belt—' He needed his gun, but could never find it. Like a man dying of thirst and clawing dirt the last few yards to water, he tore at Henny.

His two hands clamped on the gun at his face, on Henny's fingers that held it, snapping the wrist back, twisting. The wagon lurched over a rock. Henny swayed unbalanced, and the gun exploded, a deafening roar between them. Henny folded backward upon him, and Lincoln held blindly to the twisted hand. When Henny made a dead weight, and there was no more struggle, he released the grip that twisted

Henny's fist inward. The gun that had pointed into Henny's throat slid free. Henny had waited a second too long. It was almost like Henny had done it himself. Lincoln pushed free from the tangle. Fumbling into Henny's bloody shirt, he found the fastenings, loosened the money belt, and tugged it from around Henny's waist. He worked his fingers, pressuring the currency bulges, with a heady thankfulness for the remembered feel of it.

Dragging himself over into the seat was a painful process. When he had made it, with the shoulder pain throbbing anew, he groped for the lines. He got the team moving again. Dock's wagon made a swaying gray patch on the night a distance ahead.

He heard the horse loping toward him.

Claude had caught the gunshot sound. Or else was coming to check on Henny and the reason for the wagon straggling so far back.

Just Claude and Dock left now. But his strength was drained out. It was problem enough just to stay upright and hold the lines.

Claude rode up, a cautious distance out, then turned his horse, moving parallel with the wagon. Lincoln got his hand to his gun butt, on the side away from Claude. Claude peered hard up at him in the faint light.

'That's Link, ain't it? Where in hell's Henny?'

'Sleeping. I'm relieving him—'

'I heard a shot back there.'

232

'It was somewhere over in the brush.'

Claude's voice was hoarse with suspicion. 'Pull up. I'll take a look at Henny.'

'No need for that—I'm trying to catch up with Dock's wagon.'

'Pull up, damn it!'

Claude had a Colt in his right hand.

Lincoln said thickly, to divert Claude, 'Henny had my money on him. He was the one that took it—Mev Trout knew about it, somehow. He tried to bargain me for it. The bunch is falling all to pieces, Claude. You—'

'I said stop the wagon! Get both hands out there on the lines!'

Lincoln half-turned, called over his shoulder, but watching Claude, 'Get up here, Henny. Claude wants you. Wake up!'

He made his move then, in the passing moment when Claude must have dropped his caution, looking for Henny to appear. His desperation fed strength to his fingers and speed to his swing of the Colt. Claude saw this, too late. The guns roared out together. Claude's bullet ripped splinters from the wagon front. Lincoln's smashed home first, and the moonlight bathed a saddle emptied now of the Tobin he had always feared and hated the most. The riderless horse panicked and ran.

He glanced back at the dark huddle on the ground that was Claude Tobin, now beyond the last border he would ever cross. He

233

controlled the team that had tried to run with the gunshots, finally bringing the wagon to a stop. Dock's wagon showed a little distance ahead, also halted. He saw Dock climbing down over the wheel.

Weak in the legs, Lincoln made a shaky descent to the ground, steadying himself with a hand against the wheel. Dock's figure detached itself from the wagon.

Dock started toward him, and Lincoln saw that he walked strangely, yawing and weaving, his hands held out before him. He went to meet Dock.

Beyond, at the wagon, another figure, a small one, emerged. Billie walked a little way behind Dock, then stopped.

He heard her call, 'Lincoln, he's—'

'Stop there, Uncle!'

'Where are you, Link? Where's Claude?' Dock kept stumbling forward. Now he swung a gun in his hand. His big head lifted high and moved from side to side against the night.

Lincoln stared hard, almost knowing, yet disbelieving.

'Claude's dead,' he replied. 'Like Ponch and Henny. Like Coaley and Trout.'

'You kill them, boy?'

Lincoln planted himself and they stood facing each other in the moonlight, no more than twenty paces apart, with Dock seeming to search, to feel ahead. The last Tobin. He wished he did not have to kill him.

'It was you that killed them, Uncle,' he called softly. 'Back at Uvalde and Del Rio and Cottonwood, and down at Nuevo Laredo—all those men you've killed in the past. They came back, Dock. They're here tonight.'

Dock felt ahead with a booted foot. 'Talk louder, Link—I can't hear you. I can't see!'

He's gone blind! Lincoln stood frozen, watching the old man. Dock strayed to the right in his staggering walk, came against a low bush, backed away, and wagged his head helplessly.

'I can't see.'

'Drop your gun, Uncle!'

His voice helped to center Dock's attention toward him. Lincoln crouched quickly. Dock was bringing the gun up.

'This ain't no good.' Dock's lonely mumble barely came to his hearing. 'Everybody's left me. You bury me, boy—out where you buried Buckshot Withers.'

Lincoln saw Dock's last gunplay. The old Colt in the old hand centered its muzzle between the two offending eyes. One long, strained moment of silence shredded apart with the explosion of the suicide bullet. Dock sagged face down into the mesquite bush.

Billie came on from the wagon, circling wide past Dock, then ran the last little distance, and braced Lincoln as his legs gave way.

Later, as the sky showed the graying cast of dawn, she brought him water that he craved

235

and also cleansed his wounds, making a new bandage for his shoulder. By midmorning, the two wagons bobbled across the roughs, twisting between the mounds and boulders, through the mesquites, swinging southeast. Somewhere in that direction, he thought, would be Laredo. Sometime during the day, perhaps, they might be sighted by a far-ranging rider. Billie drove the second wagon, close behind him. And it was Billie, who, in late afternoon, was first covered by the rifle muzzle protruding from a split boulder beside the route.

Lincoln heard the grim command back there: 'Stop your wagon and don't move!' As he turned to peer back, a second rifle barrel fixed on him from the boulders. A voice came over: 'Pull up—climb down from there backward.'

He and Billie stood beside the wagons when the two men came out with rifles. One said, 'Keep your back turned and drop your gun to the ground.' He complied.

'Check in the wagons, Berra—Be careful.'

In a moment, the other called out, 'One dead man in here, Ray.'

'All right. You two turn around now, slow.'

Lincoln and Billie faced them. He saw two weathered men, one middle-aged, one young, both capable-looking. They gave their captives a curious study.

The younger one said, 'I'm Ray Duncan of

the Rangers. This is Sheriff Berra. You can drop your hands now.'

Lincoln had to reach for his shoulder where the blood seepage had started again. 'Glad to meet you,' he said stiffly, because he was having a hard time staying on his feet. 'I'm Link Jones—I guess you might say I'm the last of the Tobins.'

Then he added, 'This is Miss Billie Ellis.'

These were strange formalities, he thought. The glaring sun, middle of nowhere, just himself and Billie and the law standing there, all looking each other over, the two men taking him in, then Billie, then glancing at each other.

Ranger Duncan's dark features relaxed to make smile crinkles around his alert eyes. He said, 'Hell of a place to come looking for a schoolteacher, Odessa.'

Lincoln stared hard, not sure he'd heard rightly. Billie got to him first, trying to prop him as he swayed. Far away he heard her say in great exasperation, 'Will you *please* not just stand there—'

Duncan and Berra hurried to aid her. 'Yes, ma'am!' Duncan said heartily. 'Let me help you—Miss Ellis.'

*   *   *

A week later, in Laredo, Lincoln was ready to take the night train for the long journey north to Fort Worth. Ranger Duncan and Billie had called on him every day at Sheriff Berra's house. Mrs Berra had proved to be an expert nurse, and the doctor had pronounced him fit for travel. Berra had pulled strings that had landed Billie and engagement at the Border Palace where her singing was pleasing the customers nightly. On her last visit, that afternoon, Billie had managed to see him alone for a moment.

'Your eyes look mighty sparkling, for some reason,' he said. 'Been noticing it for two or three days, now. That Ranger have something to do with it?'

She touched his arm. 'Might be—I'll never forget you, Lincoln,' she murmured. 'It's all like an old nightmare, now—all but you. The rest I can forget, some day.'

'You did fine, Billie.'

She tiptoed, kissed him quickly on the mouth, and turned away. At the door, where Ranger Duncan was waiting, she faced back to him. The sparkling in her eyes had a misty look to it now.

'Good-by—*Link*!'

'So long, Billie.'

Sheriff Berra came home that night to walk to the depot with him.

'I got to wire Forth Worth that you're leaving tonight. They want you there, pretty bad.'

'Want me in Forth Worth?' Lincoln stiffened.

238

'Yeah. This fire chief. They got a fire department. Fire department's organized a band. They want to play.'

Lincoln squinted and raised one eyebrow.

'At the depot, when your train comes in.'

'Run it through the chute again, sheriff, slower.'

Berra said, 'Fort Worth's gonna welcome you. The band and the mayor and about twenty schoolteacher prospects. For what you did to clean up this Tobin business, for one thing. The other thing—' Berra fumbled in his pocket, drew out a letter and a newspaper clipping. 'Duncan's headquarters sent him this. That's when they said forget all about you ever having been the Link Jones kid with the Tobin bunch. It's the letter you wrote the school man in Fort Worth. When he heard about the big bandit chase, he had it put in the paper.'

Lincoln smoothed the clipping. Familiar words, originally written in his own hand, came back to him from the newspaper printing:

To the Head Schoolmaster
Town of Forth Worth, Texas.

Sir:
The undersigned has been elected by the citizenry of the Odessa Country to employ a schoolteacher for a school we desire to start

239

out here for our children, there being twelve prospects in number: ten white, one son of a tame Tonkawa family working on the McAlister place, and one adult man, Clabe Tiebolt, who only wants reading and writing and will pay extra by furnishing a saddle horse. I will come to Forth Worth in the month of April for that purpose and will most earnestly appreciate your esteemed favor to assist me to get in touch with a suitable prospect. This is a long way off from anywhere, but we are prepared to offer good pay, in the amount of six hundred dollars cash in hand, the same yearly thereafter, with room and meals thrown in. Man teacher preferred. If there is more than one prospect, we would prefer to make a deal with the one you think nearest meets the specifications we have adopted in public meeting, they being, to wit:

1. Foremost, that this teacher believe in the Maker and act accordingly, this being more important than anything, especially this far west in Texas, as we look on Him as the only reason we ever got by out here in the first place and want our children, including the Tonk kid, to grow up knowing that, if they never learn anything else.

2. Also, that he not be too put out about the recent folding up of the Confederacy, and should hold a right deal of pride in our State and Republic and not run the Union down, and teach respect for the Law of Texas and the

Constitution of U.S. This is a coming country.
3. It would help if he was acquainted with horses and firearms, could help on roundups and branding in rush seasons, and not be stampeded by sight of a few Indians, but this Odessa section is taming up.
4. Anything else he knew to teach would be that much extra advantage, especially reading, writing, and some arithmetic.

I will do myself the privilege of presuming to make your acquaintance upon my arrival in your city and will appreciate your help in my mission.

Yr. Obd Srvnt.
Lincoln Jones

Attest:

Fez Duncan
J. D. Clinkscale
Committee.

He folded the clipping and handed it back to Berra.

A band, Berra had said. At the depot. A strange lot of fuss. But right nice, he guessed. He tried to visualize such an arrival. 'Gosh—this Sunday suit,' he said. 'It's been wadded up in my valise. You know somebody I could get to iron out the wrinkles before I leave?'

'Stay put.' Berra stood. 'My wife's the best suit ironer I know.' He went to the back of the house to find her.

The suit soon looked real smooth, suitable for a long train ride, for getting off in Forth Worth where there would be all the commotion with a band, and twenty schoolteachers. Walking to the train with Berra, his valise tightly held in his left hand, money belt tight around his lean middle, six-gun snug under his coat, his deep prairieman's eyes squinting ahead, he felt a tug on his arm as they passed the front of the Border Palace.

'Take a look in here a minute,' Berra said. 'Want to show you something.'

They stood in the crowd in the darkened back part of the house, and waited until Billie Ellis came on the small stage. She was pretty as a picture, Lincoln thought, in a ruffly pink dress, her face and hair fixed nice, her smile bright and sassy, and the crowd was applauding her like everything. The piano struck up a lively introduction. And Billie sang.

Ten rollicking stanzas about the cowboy and the girl and the brindle bull. She went off blowing kisses and the men yelled and stomped and cheered. Billie had to come back for four bows and on the final one, Lincoln and Berra saw her throw the last kiss straight down to the first table.

'Look at this!' Berra nudged him. 'He's been there every night.'

Ranger Ray Duncan was the man who

caught the kiss, and came to his feet and clapped his hands long after Billie had gone and the curtain was down. Then Duncan moved through the crowd toward the door that led backstage, walking purposefully, like a man who knew where he was going. Lincoln felt Berra's elbow nudge him again.

'Beats all,' Berra murmured.

It sure did, Lincoln agreed. Berra said, 'Ray's a fine man.'

And Lincoln said at the same time, 'Billie's a fine woman.'

With both granting that *that* was settled, they continued to the train, shook hands, and Lincoln went aboard the growling, puffing contraption. He settled into a stiff plush seat in the lamplit coach, swinging his valise to the rack overhead, as Sam Beasley had shown him, like an old-time train traveler who was familiar with how to do things. Later in the night, when the train heaved and rattled northward through the dark country, he sleepily heard the conductor bawl, 'Buffalo Gap wood stop coming up—all able-bodied men help carry wood for the engine—more that help, quicker we get movin' again—' Lincoln smiled to himself and shut his eyes again and tried to recapture the misty dream he'd had working, of Lucy and the children and the clean, free breezes of the Odessa frontier in springtime. When they got to the Buffalo Gap wood stop,

243

maybe he would wake up enough to help carry mesquite for the engine, and again, maybe he wouldn't. Depended on what Lucy was saying in the dream at the time.

Will C. Brown is the pen name under which Clarence Scott Boyles, Jr., has written most of his Western fiction. Born in Baird, Texas, and descended from Texas cattle-raising families on both sides, Boyles's early career was in newspaper journalism. Although he did publish a couple of Western stories in pulp magazines in the 1930s, it was first following his discharge from the U.S. Marine Corps after the Second World War that he began his writing career in earnest. Texas is the principal setting in nearly all of Boyles's Western stories, including his first novel, THE BORDER JUMPERS (1955), which also served as the basis for the memorable motion picture, MAN OF THE WEST (1958) starring Gary Cooper. Dell Publishing, which reprinted this novel, selected it to receive the Dell Book Award as the best Western novel of 1955. THE NAMELESS BREED (1960) won the Golden Spur Award from the Western Writers of America in the category of best Western novel and is still considered to be Will C. Brown's *magnum opus*. A trek through the mile-wide *Valle de Cuchillos*, or Valley of the Knives, is the highlight of this story, vividly and harrowingly told. In these novels, as well as in LAREDO ROAD (1959), CAPROCK REBEL (1962), and THE KELLY MAN (1964), a high level of suspense is established early and maintained throughout, often by characters being pitted against adverse elements and terrain. Boyles is particularly adept at making his readers feel the heat, dust, wind, desolation, deprivation, and dangers of the land in his stories. When violence does occur, it is logical and handled with restraint and brevity.

We hope you have enjoyed this Large Print book. Other Chivers Press or G. K. Hall Large Print books are available at your library or directly from the publishers. For more information about current and forthcoming titles, please call or write, without obligation, to:

Chivers Press Limited
Windsor Bridge Road
Bath BA2 3AX
England
Tel. (01225) 335336

OR

G. K. Hall
P.O. Box 159
Thorndike, Maine 04986
USA
Tel. (800) 223–6121 (U.S. & Canada)
In Maine call collect: (207) 948–2962

All our Large Print titles are designed for easy reading, and all our books are made to last.